HAUNTED
and
Revered

THE SCOTSMAN'S DESTINED LOVE

BY
BREE WOLF

BREE WOLF
author

Cover Art by Victoria Cooper
Copyright © 2019 Bree Wolf

Paperback ISBN: 978-3-96482-060-0
Hard Cover ISBN: 978-3-96482-106-5

www.breewolf.com

To Our Children

Acknowledgments

A great, big thank-you to my dedicated beta readers and proofreaders, Michelle Chenoweth, Monique Takens and Kim Bougher, who read the rough draft and help me make it better.

Also a heartfelt thank-you to all my wonderful readers who pick up book after book and follow me on these exciting adventures of love and family. I love your company and savor every word of your amazing reviews! Thank you so much! There are no words!

HAUNTED
and
Revered

THE SCOTSMAN'S DESTINED LOVE

Prologue

Greystone Castle, Scotland

Autumn 1809

"Will nothing keep you from your little sanctuary? Not even the child in your belly?"

Standing on a small ladder, Deidre Brunwood felt her hand pause as she heard Henrietta's voice call out to her, a teasing chuckle following her words as the tall woman stepped out of the thick hedge growing around the small, lost garden Deidre had made her own.

Situated between the outer wall and the castle wall itself, it could only be reached through a small gap in the tall-growing hedge. A gap one could not see if one did not know where to look. Untended for years, it had grown wild, and Deidre remembered well the day she had first stumbled upon it, an oasis of greens of all shades mingling with bright yellows, dark reds and stunning violets. Her soul had soared to the heavens upon seeing it, and Deidre had known in that moment that she had found a piece of her heart.

"Why don't you ask someone to help you with the apple harvest?" Henrietta suggested as she came walking over, her short flaxen hair dancing upon her shoulders. She bore a tall, striking figure despite her slender build, an Englishwoman by birth, but a Scot at heart. Married to Deidre's cousin Connor, Laird of Clan Brunwood, Henrietta had been a close friend for many years.

"Mama, fwower!" Henrietta's two-year-old daughter Bridget exclaimed, pulling on her mother's skirts and pointing at a pale rose, still blooming this late in the year. Her blond hair shone as brightly as her mother's, and her deep blue eyes whispered of a daring spirit eagerly reaching for the wonders the world promised her.

Smiling, Henrietta brushed a hand over Bridget's head as she shifted her balance to accommodate baby Aileen, who lay sleeping peacefully in the crook of her other arm. At three-month-old, Aileen knew nothing of what her big sister spoke so ardently. Her little head sprouted dark brown curls, and her eyes glowed in a striking green whenever she dared to open them, her little heart far more content to look inward than to face the world. The girls were like fire and water, different in temperament and appearance, but the glow on their little faces never failed to make Deidre's heart ache.

Plucking the apple she had been reaching for, Deidre climbed down the ladder and laid it down in the basket that was already half-full. "I find it soothing," she told her friend as her hand came to rest upon the small bulge under her dress.

Henrietta stepped closer, the look in her blue eyes tense. "Are you not worried that it might...?" her voice trailed off as her gaze dipped lower to where Deidre's hand rested protectively over her unborn child.

Deidre swallowed as she remembered the many pregnancies that had ended in loss. "I dunna believe it makes a difference. I've stayed abed before, and it didna help." Her insides clenched. "I still lost my babe." Her hand brushed softly over her belly. "I believe the best I can do is to not be afraid to live and smile and laugh as much as I can. I dunna know whether I'm meant to hold this babe in my arms or not, but I will love every moment I have with him or her." Tears filled her eyes, but Deidre quickly blinked them away. She had already shed a lifetime's worth of tears over the loss of her children, not one of whom had ever drawn a breath. She would not cry today when there was no reason to do so.

Drawing in a deep breath, Deidre lifted her head, willing the sadness back down. "What brings ye here? Have ye come to lend a hand?"

Henrietta chuckled, glancing at Bridget chasing after a butterfly, her little legs carrying her through the tall grass. "I'm afraid all my hands are currently occupied," she said, rocking little Aileen as the girl began to stir. A soft melody drifted from her lips as she hummed, brushing the pad of her thumb over her daughter's crinkled forehead, soothing the sorrows that had found her in her dreams until the little girl slept peacefully once more.

A lump settled in Deidre's throat as longing tugged on her heart yet again. She loved Henrietta's children dearly, but they only strengthened the yearning for a child of her own.

"I brought you this," Henrietta whispered, reaching into her apron and withdrawing a letter. "It was delivered this morning, and I've been looking for you ever since." Her blue eyes met Deidre's. "It came from *Seann Dachaigh* Tower."

"Moira?" Deidre asked, her hand reaching out for the envelope.

Henrietta nodded. "It seems to be her handwriting if I'm not mistaken." Her jaw tensed at the mention of the woman who had tried to steal her husband. "Connor confirmed it."

Deidre nodded, her gaze gliding over Moira's flourished handwriting. They had been friends since childhood, and they had grown closer still when Deidre had married Moira's elder brother Alastair. Nothing had ever come between them until the day Moira had gone too far.

For her betrayal, she had been banished from her home, sent to live with her mother's old clan at *Seann Dachaigh* Tower. Life had not been easy for her, but Moira had come to see the error of her ways and fought hard to make amends and regain people's trust. Ultimately, her devotion and loyalty to Clan MacDrummond had won her the laird's heart, and they had been married only a few weeks past. Still, Alastair had never forgiven his sister for her betrayal, and ever since, Deidre had stood in the middle, trying her best to mend fences.

Breaking the seal, Deidre opened the envelope and pulled out a single sheet of parchment. She unfolded it, her eyes drawn to the words written there as an odd sense of foreboding fell over her.

Dearest Deirdre,

This is not an easy letter to write for I fear I must warn you of something that lies ahead. I will do my best to share with you all that I know, but I'm afraid the images I saw were shrouded as though hidden in a heavy fog. You will have to trust your heart to guide you as do I for I know that there is no better compass than the gentle soul that resides within you.

Deidre's blood ran cold at Moira's words.

Three months ago when she had first learned that she was with child, Deidre had travelled to *Seann Dachaigh* Tower to speak to Moira, to ask her if she knew what fate her unborn child was destined for. Would it live? Or would she lose it as she had lost all the others?

Ever since she had been a lass, Moira'd had the Sight. Dreams that whispered of future events: some clear and some shrouded in mist, impossible to understand until they came to pass. One such dream had led her to conspire against Connor's and Henrietta's marriage. A dream she had misunderstood.

As hopeful as Deidre tried to be, she could not deny that she feared for her child's life. How could she not? And so, she had gone to Moira asking for help. Only Moira had not been able to tell her anything as no dream whispering of her child's future had yet found her. Still, Moira had promised to write should anything change. Should she see anything in her dreams.

Deidre felt her hands begin to tremble.

"Are you all right?" Henrietta asked, her voice full of concern as she came to stand by Deidre, her unburdened arm coming around her friend's shoulders. "You've gone awfully pale. What does she write? Is everything all right?"

Unable to speak, Deidre held up the letter, gesturing for Henrietta to read along.

The images that found me were blurred and shifted quickly, and I'm afraid I'm far from certain as to their meaning. I pray you will be able to make more sense of them.

At first, I found myself looking upon a blue flower, its petals strangely tined and not smooth but as though wrinkled. The colour moved and shifted into different shades in stark contrast to the bright light surrounding it. I felt blinded, my eyes seeing nothing but white.

As far as I can tell the flower is nothing more but a marker. It marks the day when something will come to pass. As to what that is, I cannot say for certain. All I know is that I saw you up on the cliffs by the old ruins, brightness around you. A sense of utter sadness washed over me, making my heart ache. Still, it only lingered for a short while before suddenly, my heart felt ready to burst with a new love.

"A new love?" Henrietta whispered beside her. "What does she mean?"

Deidre shook her head, her heart torn. "I dunna know." She had expected news about her child, and yet, Moira's words spoke of something else. Could this be about her husband? About Alastair?

As you well know, my interpretation of these dreams is not free of error. I do not know what will happen. I can merely speculate.

Of course, I worry about what they could mean for I cannot deny that the images I saw echoed with warning. However, I've recently come to understand that my ability to interpret these dreams is less accurate whenever I myself am emotionally involved. If that is the case, I can no longer be objective, and my interpretation becomes flawed.

I love you as I would my own sister, dearest Deidre, and so I fear that I'm not of much help. All I can tell you is that on the day marked by the blue flower, you're to seek out the old ruins, and there you will stumble upon a great love.

I will not say more and will leave all else in your trusted hands.

5

Be safe.

Moira

By the time, Deidre reached the end of the letter, her limbs were shaking so hard, she sank down into the leaf-covered grass, Henrietta beside her. Her eyes closed, and one hand reached out to her unborn child as her mind pictured her beloved husband.

Was that what Moira had been reluctant to say? That harm would befall Alastair? That at some point in the future, Deidre would stumble upon a new love.

"Impossible," she whispered into the stillness of her sanctuary, feeling Henrietta's arm tighten upon her shoulders. "Even if..." Her eyes opened, and she felt tears run down her cheeks as she turned to look upon her friend. "Even if he were..." Deidre swallowed. "I could never give my heart to another. Never."

Blinking back tears, Henrietta nodded, her hand seeking Deidre's squeezing it gently. "I know," she whispered, then cleared her throat, casting a watchful look at Aileen. "Perhaps Moira is wrong." Her jaw tensed. "After all, she's been wrong before. Perhaps whatever she saw will not happen to you, but to another."

Deidre nodded, wishing she could grasp the lifeline Henrietta was offering her. Still, she knew that if Moira had not been certain, she would not have written this letter. Like no other, Moira knew the bond that connected Deidre and Alastair, the love that had bound them to one another ever since they had been children.

It was unbreakable.

Forever.

Destined.

"Will you tell Alastair about this?" Henrietta asked, aware of the tension between brother and sister. Even though Deidre had all but forced her husband to follow her when she had slipped away to *Seann Dachaigh* Tower three months ago, brother and sister had barely spoken a word to each other when he had arrived to fetch his wife home. Alastair still had not forgiven Moira. Could not.

He was a proud man.

Stubborn.

Unyielding.

"'Twill only anger him," Deidre said, knowing from the look in Henrietta's eyes that her friend agreed. "He'll be furious with her, and it'll push them even farther apart." She sighed, feeling exhausted. "I still have hope that one day they'll find their way back to each other."

Henrietta swallowed, the look in her eyes wary. "What about...your new love? The man you will meet by the ruins?"

Deidre shook her head. "I dunna care. My heart belongs to Alastair. It always has, and it always will."

A smile came to Henrietta's face, and she squeezed Deidre's hand. "There's not a single doubt-"

"None!" Her heart beat strong, and yet, her jaw quivered. "But what if...?" Both her hands reached for Henrietta's. "What if harm comes to him? What if that's the warning Moira felt? What do I do?"

Henrietta heaved a deep sigh before her gaze moved from the letter in Deidre's lap to the small bump under her dress. "It is as you said, you do not know what will happen. None of us do. All any of us can do is be happy and enjoy the time we have. What else is there?"

Deidre nodded, knowing Henrietta was right. Still, a new fear settled in her heart, and she knew it would haunt her for all the days to come. The fear to not only lose her child, but also to keep her husband as well. For although nothing could ever make her love another, her heart would break into a thousand pieces, never to be mended again, if Fate dared to separate her from the man she loved.

Chapter One
A LOOMING THREAT

Greystone Castle, Scotland
Winter 1811

Two Years Later

S now fell heavily upon the old ruins, hiding the ancient boulders under a blanket of white, glittering frost. The winds blew strong, carrying the tiny flakes on swift wings, swirling them in the air before allowing them to settle in peace. The cliff top fell away sharply not far from where Deidre stood in the deep snow, waves crashing below, the sea a raging monster, snarling and spitting.

Her feet were warm in the fur-lined boots she wore, and her cloak held off the sharp sting of the ice-cold wind. Still, her cheeks burnt from the icy needles assaulting her skin, and she knew she could not linger here much longer.

And yet, her heart ached at the thought of leaving this place.

Ever since the day Fate had taken yet another child from her, Deidre had somehow found her way to this spot. Again and again.

Why, she could not say.

Spring had been well on its way when Deidre had woken one

morning to find her little daughter lying still and cold in her crib. For a desperate moment, Deidre had believed her asleep, her blue eyes closed in peaceful slumber, the red tuft of hair on her head as wild and unruly as ever.

Rory, they had called her when she had been born three months before. *Rory, the red-haired lass.*

A promise of happiness.

Of a future longed for with all her heart and soul.

Of love and family.

And then her precious child had been gone.

No longer did Deidre hear the soft cooing sounds when Rory wanted to nurse. No longer did she wake in the night to find her daughter fast asleep, an innocent smile tickling her face. No longer did she feel her child's warm body in her arms, a comfort and joy if ever she had known one.

No longer.

It had all come to an end far, far too soon.

A year and a half had passed since they buried Rory, and sometimes Deidre still felt detached from the world around her. More often than not during the first year after their loss, her heart had felt numb, unable to produce any emotion except for the soul-crushing pain that lingered as though determined to make her suffer, forcing tears from her eyes that seemed to know no end.

Alastair too had been a mere shadow of himself. However, unlike Deidre, he had not retreated, had not shied away from those around him. Instead, his face had been stoic, his eyes all but dead; yet, he had moved among the living as though nothing had happened.

There in body, but not in heart and soul.

And while Deidre had found a way to feel again, to return from the black abyss her daughter's loss had thrown her into, Alastair was still lost. They had not only lost their child, but also each other. Before, when a pregnancy had ended early, they had turned to one another, sharing their pain and finding comfort in each other's arms.

But after Rory's death, they both had fallen apart, lost to each other, unable to connect, their bond thinning with each day that passed.

Would it snap eventually?

Cold fear gripped Deidre at the thought, and a part of her wished the dam around her husband's heart would finally break, freeing the torrent of pain and sorrow that lived within, while another part of her feared that should it truly break, he would never be able to recover. That she would lose him for good.

Was that the warning Moira had felt in her dream two years ago? The loss of one another? Hearts broken beyond repair?

Oddly enough, through all the heartache she had suffered in the past year and a half, that thought gave Deidre strength. For it told her that there was a way back. That all was not lost.

Aye, she had lost her child. There had been nothing she could have done to save Rory. Deidre knew that even though it did not lessen the pain. However, she would be damned if she lost her husband as well. For him, she *could* fight.

And she would.

And so, every day, Deidre looked for the blue flower Moira had written to her about, wondering when the marked day would finally arrive, hoping with all her heart and soul that the threat of another's love would eventually shake Alastair awake.

Would he fight for her if his place in her heart were threatened by another? Not that that could ever happen.

Still, sometimes doubt was good. Sometimes it helped to make one see more clearly. Sometimes, it could shake one awake.

For she wanted him back. She needed him back.

And he needed her as well even if he was too stubborn to admit it.

So, Deidre often rode to the ruins that sat atop the tall cliff face, not truly expecting to find anything or anyone, but only to have a moment to herself. To remember her beloved child. To gain strength for the fight ahead. To remind herself not to give up.

Inhaling an ice-cold breath, Deidre tugged the hood tighter around her head and then turned, heading back to the only remaining part of the old ruins that still offered some shelter. There she had left her trusted mare, Aurora, out of the chilling wind as the sturdy walls and the remnant ceiling held it at bay.

Mumbling words of comfort to the white mare, her coat a perfect match for the snow-covered hills around them, Deidre wrapped her arms around the animal's neck, enjoying the comfort of her warmth. A soft nicker answered her, and Deidre smiled into Aurora's soft coat. "Aye, 'tis cold. We should head back."

Stepping back, she reached for the reins when a shadow fell over her from behind. Her breath lodged in her throat, and Deidre spun around, her eyes wide as they fixed on the dim outline of someone walking toward her through the swirling snow.

Panic surged through her heart, and it hammered wildly against her ribs as she backed away.

"Deidre!"

At the sound of her husband's voice, Deidre's knees almost buckled in relief, and for a short second she closed her eyes, leaning her forehead against her mare's neck. "'Tis only Alastair," she whispered as though it had been her trusted mount that had been spooked.

A moment later, a tall, broad-shouldered man stepped into the small space sheltered from the outdoors. His boots were encrusted with snow, and his coat looked almost white with the myriad of tiny flakes clinging to it. He pushed back his hood, revealing his dark blond hair tied in the back as well as his piercing blue eyes, eyes that had always been full of tenderness when they had looked into hers.

Now, they reminded her of an icy lake, frosted over and treacherous. Dull and cold and distant as they could not see what was right in front of them.

"What are ye doing out here?" His gaze shifted over her, lingering on her reddened cheeks instead of her eyes. "Surely, ye must be mad to seek out this place in such weather." His jaw clenched, and despite his rough demeanour, Deidre could see the tension that held him. He had been concerned for her. He had followed her because he cared. He no longer told her so, but she knew it to be true.

Still, the distance that lingered between them sent a chill through her heart that not even the freezing coldness of a winter's day could match. "I came here to think," she told him as she stepped closer, her eyes seeking his. "To remember our daughter."

Instantly, he shied away. His gaze dropped from hers, and he shuffled backwards, his teeth clenched. "Ye can do so in the safety of Greystone Castle. Let's head back."

As he made to leave, Deidre reached out and grasped the front of his coat, pulling him back, determined not to let him leave. Not like this. Not today.

That morning, she had not woken determined to seize this day in such a daring way; however, her heart told her in that moment that she had very little to lose. "There's something I need to tell ye."

His blue eyes dropped to her hand where it still rested against his chest, her fingers curled into the fabric of his coat. Then they rose to meet hers, and for a bare moment, Deidre saw something old flicker to life there, and she knew a part of him still remembered what they had once had and longed to have it back the same as she did herself.

"About two years ago," Deidre began, her skin crawling with fear as well as excitement to have finally reached this moment so unexpectedly, "I received a letter."

Alastair's gaze narrowed, and his shoulders pulled back as though to force more distance between them.

In answer, Deidre's grip tightened. "'Twas from yer sister."

Anger flared to life in her husband's eyes, and he made to shrug her off. "I'll not speak about her."

"But I will!" Deidre insisted, holding on tight, her gaze hardening to match her husband's. She did not care that he towered over her like a giant. He had never frightened her. Not in that way. What frightened her now was the coldness that seemed to claim his heart a little more each day. A coldness that little by little replaced the love he had always had for her.

Once, his heart had been hers, and she wanted it back.

"She wrote to me about a dream she'd had."

Alastair's lips thinned for although he had always disliked his sister's ability, he knew as well as Deidre did that it was real, and he had always feared it for it made him feel powerless. A worse feeling Alastair had never known; a feeling he was well-acquainted with as he had held her hand through countless miscarriages, unable to help, to take the pain, to soothe the loss.

Aye, he knew the feeling well, and the hard line of his jaw told her that he was determined not to allow it into his heart again. Was that why he was pushing her away?

Deidre inhaled a deep breath, the thought to add pain to his heart settling like ice into every fibre of her being. "She wrote that on the day marked by a blue flower, I'd find a great love up here by the ruins." The words flew from her lips as she forced herself to hold his gaze.

Although her husband barely moved, Deidre could see the shock that gripped him, clutched him in an iron vice, cutting off air and warmth and stirring pain and sorrow anew. Jealousy flared in his eyes, and anger surged through his muscles as his hands flew forward, gripping her arms. He hauled her against him, bringing her face closer to his, his warm breath brushing over her chilled skin as his blue eyes burnt into hers. "Is that why ye're here?" he snarled. "D'ye want to run off?"

Deidre rejoiced at the emotions she saw, proof that the passionate man her husband had always been was still there, deep inside. "I havena yet seen the blue flower," she told him, her chin quivering as she held her breath, fighting not to let him see how much his reaction pleased her. If he caught a glimpse of the game she was playing, would he banish her from his heart for good?

His grip tightened. "Then why are ye up here?" he growled, his arms all but lifting her off the ground as he pulled her closer still. "Are ye hoping the bastard will find ye here?" He shook her as his voice rasped with rage. "D'ye intend to leave?"

His lips almost touched hers, and Deidre could feel her breath come fast as her blood boiled with emotions she had not felt in a long time. In too long. "Would ye let me go?" she dared him, striving closer to brush her lips against his, nothing more but a feather-light touch, but it shot through him like a bolt of lightning.

His eyes drilled into hers, and for a moment, Deidre found herself looking at the man she had married so long ago. Tears misted her eyes, and a gasp was torn from her lips when he suddenly crushed her into his arms, his mouth closing over hers.

Passion flared as Alastair kissed her with an almost desperate need, like a man drowning afraid to let go, afraid to lose the one he loved the most. Emotions buried under a thick layer of ice fought to the surface and fuelled his blood, breaking down all the barriers he had set up over the course of the past year and a half.

Deidre was swept away by the power of his response. Her head spun as she clung to him, and she felt shivers dance along her skin where his hands reached under her cloak, feeling her through the thinner fabric of her dress.

Awakening, her body responded to him with a fierceness Deidre had all but forgotten, and she kissed him back, her hands striving to hold him closer. Not since they had lost their child had he held her like this, kissed her like this. The day they had lost Rory, they had also lost each other.

But no more.

Deidre wanted him back.

She needed him back.

And he needed her.

As the snow swirled around them, Deidre sank into her husband's arms, for the first time in so long feeling a shred of hope, of happiness, an echo of the past, long since lost and forgotten. Still, somewhere deep down, her heart remembered. "I want ye," she whispered against his lips as her fingers moved down his neck and slipped inside his coat finding warm skin.

Alastair froze.

Chapter Two

A MAN'S WEAKNESS

Deidre's touch almost brought him to his knees, so achingly sweet and familiar, comforting and desperately alluring. He had craved her ever since stealing a first kiss when she had been but a young lass. He had wanted her then, and he wanted her now. His blood hummed when she was near, and when those soft brown eyes looked into his, his resolve wavered and fled, and he found himself unable to deny her anything. She was his weakness, his heart and soul, the very breath of his body...

...and he had brought her nothing but pain and loss.

Bowing his head, Alastair stepped away, his hands sliding from her warm body and falling into fists at his side. He ought to have listened to his parents that day long years ago when they had warned him, told him to choose another, a woman strong enough to bear his children. He had always been tall and broad while Deidre had always been delicate, her head reaching no higher than halfway up his chest, her frame dainty, almost fragile.

His parents had warned him, but he had not listened. He had been in love, and he had thought he knew better.

But he had been wrong.

And it had cost her dearly. She would have been better off with another. Perhaps Moira's vision was Fate's way of urging him to finally let her go. Perhaps she could still find happiness.

But not with him.

Still, the thought of Deidre in the arms of another felt like a boulder crushing his heart. His chest felt constricted as though he could no longer draw breath, and a freezing cold slowly spread through his body, chasing away the warm glow her touch had left behind.

"Fight for me."

At the fierceness in her voice, Alastair looked up, his eyes drawn to the soft glow of her cheeks, the determined set of her jaw, the silent plea in her soulful eyes. The warmth of her skin still lingered on his, and he remembered well the way she had felt in his arms. It had been too long since he last held her, and it had not been enough.

He wanted more.

He wanted what they had once had.

Moving towards him, Deidre reached out and her dainty hands settled back on his chest. "Look at me."

Even through the layers of clothing, Alastair could feel her and the fierceness of his longing for her grew. Never had he been able to stay away from her. To be near her and not touch her. "We should head back."

"Look at me!" his wife urged, anger lacing her voice as her fingers once more curled into his coat.

Alastair loved the strength that lived within her. Never had she cowered in the face of one of his thunderous outbursts. Never had she backed down or bowed her head. She possessed a fierce spirit, his little wife!

"Do you want me to go?" Deidre finally asked, her brown eyes misted with tears as she looked up at him. "Do you no longer want me?" A sob escaped her lips, and Alastair's heart broke into a thousand pieces at the sight of her sorrow.

"If what Moira saw is true," he replied through gritted teeth, fighting the urge to haul her back into his arms and kiss away her tears, "then it doesna matter what I want." He shifted backwards, and her hands dropped from his chest. "Perhaps we should never have been. Perhaps our union was against Fate's will. Perhaps 'tis why we," he tried to swallow the lump in his throat, "keep losing our children."

Air rushed from her lungs in a painful sob, and for a moment, Alastair feared she would break down. "How can ye say that? D'ye truly wish we lived in a world where Rory had never been? Can ye truly imagine never having known her?"

Tears shot to Alastair's eyes at the thought of his wee lassie, and he spun on his heel, determined to hide them. "Get on yer horse," he snapped. "We're heading back." Then he stalked from the small shelter to where he had left his own mount and pulled himself into the saddle. His midnight-black gelding pranced nervously, voicing his displeasure at having been left out in the swirling snow.

Pausing, Alastair reached inside his coat and pulled out a curl of soft auburn-red hair tied with a blue velvet ribbon. With one hand on the reins, he hunched over, shielding his precious treasure from the snow, before running his eyes over the small tuft of hair.

At the mere sight of his daughter's lock, his heart ached with a fierceness that nearly had him topple over in pain. Again, he saw Rory's gentle smile as she slept peacefully in his arms. Again, he felt her small hand grip his finger and hold it with a strength that had taken his breath away. Again, he felt his heart swell with pride and love at the mere sight of her.

Never could he imagine a world without her. And yet, the memory of her made life a burden he no longer knew how to bear.

The moment Deidre urged her mare back out into the snow, Alastair quickly slipped his daughter's curl back into his coat, then turned his gelding toward home. In silence, they made their way back, each step a deafening sound that ripped the gap between them open farther. A gap Alastair knew not how to bridge and now wondered if he even should.

Surely, losing Deidre to another would rip his heart from his body; however, it was a price he would gladly pay to see her happy once more. After all, it was her only chance.

When they finally reached Greystone Castle, their horses' hooves sounding strangely dull on the snow-covered cobblestones of the courtyard, Alastair found his gaze drawn to two carriages pulled up by the front door. By the looks of it, they had only just arrived for he spotted his cousin Connor and his English wife Henrietta hurrying down the steps to welcome their visitors.

Dismounting, Alastair handed the reins to a stable boy before turning to assist his wife. To his relief as well as regret, she had already jumped down, patting Aurora before entrusting her to another stable boy. "Are those Beth and Tristan?" she asked, referring to Henrietta's brother and his wife, who had begun the tradition of spending the Yuletide season in Scotland a few years back. "I've been wondering if they would make it this year with all the snow coming down."

After a moment of hesitation, Alastair offered his wife his arm, feeling his heart pause when she slipped her dainty little hand through the crook of his arm, pulling herself close. The soft scent of roses drifted into his nose as she walked beside him, her warmth melting the ice from his weary bones.

Alastair wanted nothing more than to haul her into his arms and kiss her breathless.

But he knew, he should not.

Instead, he escorted her around the snow-covered carriages to greet their visitors.

Tristan and Beth, Lord and Lady Elton, were both tall and fair as was their daughter Ellen, who was about the same age as Bridget. The moment the two girls spotted one another, excited squeals echoed across the courtyard before they embraced each other fiercely, then dashed off to seek out new adventures. Their parents laughed before Connor and Henrietta as well as Connor's mother Rhona stepped forward to greet the little boy Beth held in her arms, her almost one-year-old son Dane, who had been born right here in Greystone Castle the year before.

Alastair felt his wife tense beside him, and when he looked down, he found her gaze misted with tears as she looked at the red-cheeked child.

Squealing in fright, Dane turned his head into his mother's shoulder when Connor approached him, his bear-like stature and thick, black beard frightening the small boy. Still, a moment later, he was already giggling with joy as the Laird of Clan Brunwood did his best to win him over, making funny faces accompanied by odd sounds.

Everyone laughed, embracing one another after the long time apart.

"Who else did ye bring?" Connor enquired, a hint of surprise in his voice, as the door to the other carriage opened and more people filed out into the courtyard.

"I hope you don't mind," Beth answered, a gentle smile on her kind face, "but I've invited my half-sister Lady Whitworth and her family as well as my half-brother Lord Radcliff and his daughter to join us this year." After gesturing to her family, Beth turned back to smile at Connor. "I thought the more the merrier."

Connor laughed, his hand reaching out to pull Henrietta into his arms with an ease that Alastair could not help but envy. "Aye, ye know me well, dear Beth, but if ye dunna mind, let's forget about the lord-and-lady nonsense." He glanced past her at his surprise guests. "I'll never remember it."

Warm smiles met him as he strode forward, greeting each one of them, asking their names and giving his own. For even though Connor Brunwood was not only the Laird of Clan Brunwood but also held the title of the Marquis of Rodridge, he was a man who did not stand on ceremony. He valued family above all and cherished the bond that came with using another's given name instead of their title.

Joining in, Alastair and Deidre greeted Matthew and Adelaide, their two-year-old son Jonathan as well as John and his seven-year-old daughter Mathilda, all a bit weary from their long journey, but all excited to be here. They were accompanied by a rather pale-looking governess by the name of Miss Harmon-or Sophie-who seemed a bit short of breath for someone who had spent the better part of the past few days seated in a carriage.

As the snow kept coming down, greetings were cut short, and everyone bustled inside the great hall of Greystone Castle where a fire in the large hearth cast its warm glow over everyone. Hot tea was served as the adults seated themselves near the stone fireplace while the children raced around the room, their little limbs buzzing with energy after being cooped up in the carriage for too long.

With a sigh, Moira left his side to sit with the women, her gaze straying to the children playing nearby again and again. Alastair knew how she felt for he too felt a stab of pain every time he saw a father pick up his child and plant a kiss on its head. Although he knew it would only bring him sorrow, he could not bring himself not to look at Tristan as he bounced Dane in his arms or to watch how Matthew swung his two-year-old son Jonathan into the air.

Rory would have been almost two years old by now. She would have been able to walk and talk, her auburn curls framing a mischievous face as she chased with the others around the hall. Oh, why could she not be here with them like all the others!

The look in Deidre's eyes whispered of the same thoughts, and as their gazes met across the room, Alastair wanted nothing more than to draw her into his arms and bury his face in her hair. He wanted to feel her arms come around him, her warm body pressed to his, and mourn that which would never be.

With her.

Together.

"I see ye found her," Connor observed as he came to stand beside him.

Not bothering to look at his cousin, Alastair merely nodded.

"Where was she?"

Alastair swallowed, "By the old ruins."

A frown came to Connor's face as he turned to look at Alastair. "She's gone there a lot this past year, has she not?"

Alastair's teeth gritted together. "Aye."

Connor's gaze narrowed. "What happened? Are ye all right?"

Knowing his cousin would not walk away unless he received the answer he sought, Alastair sighed. "She told me that," his mouth felt suddenly dry, "two years ago, Moira sent her a letter."

"Ah," was all Connor said.

Shock slammed into Alastair as he stared at his cousin. "Ye knew?"

Gritting his teeth, Connor shrugged, a hint of regret in his eyes. "Henrietta was there when she received it."

Alastair felt his jaw clench painfully. Apparently, everyone had known but him!

"I'm sorry," Connor said, putting a hand on Alastair's shoulder. "We meant no harm, least of all Deidre. She was only worried 'twould push ye and Moira even farther apart. She meant well."

Unable to think about his sister then and there, Alastair shrugged off Connor's hand. "D'ye believe it to be true?" he asked after a while, not certain which answer he hoped to receive.

Connor sighed, "I believe there's truth in these visions, but I dunna believe they tell the whole story. Ye know better than anyone that Moira has been wrong before, that she misunderstood what she'd seen."

"And yet," Alastair began as he turned to meet his friend's gaze, "'twas yer own mother's vision which sent ye to England to find Henrietta, was it not? Everything came to pass exactly as she'd seen it, did it not?" The thought that no matter what he did, he would lose his wife's love to another was utterly crippling!

Connor frowned. "D'ye truly believe yer wife could ever love another?"

"Perhaps she should."

Connor's hands grasped his shoulders. "Are ye mad? Deidre loves ye. The lass always has. Why would ye push her away? Ye're being cruel. Can ye not see how much she needs ye?"

Closing his eyes briefly, Alastair inhaled a deep breath as exhaustion washed over him. "Perhaps we were wrong. Perhaps we were never meant for one another." He swallowed, staring back into his cousin's shocked face. "Perhaps she would've found happiness with another, had a child that lived." His heart screamed out in pain. "Perhaps she still can."

"Ye canna truly believe that!"

In truth, every fibre of his being cried out in protest, but did that truly make it wrong? Was love not supposed to be selfless? If there was a chance for Deidre to find happiness, was he not bound to do what was necessary to ensure she would find it?

"Dunna tell me she goes up there because she's waiting for Moira's vision to come true?" Connor said, his dark eyes watchful and full of doubt.

Alastair shrugged. "I dunna know."

"She's yer wife!" Connor exclaimed in a strangled whisper, his gaze darting around the room, ensuring that no one was within earshot. "Fight for her!"

Fight for me!

Had Deidre not asked him to do so as well? Aye, she did love him, but was this love wise? So far, it had led them down a painful path, and perhaps now it was time to step off it. His gaze moved across the hall and met Deidre's, her soft brown eyes glowing in the warm light from the hearth.

A breath shuddered through Alastair's body at the sight, and deep longing settled in his bones. He knew it well for he had been fighting it for the better part of a year. Aye, he loved his wife. He always had, but he also feared where that love would lead them.

No longer was he strong enough to see her in pain again. To see her lose another child. To see her body exhausted and broken, slipping away, too weak to go on. More than once, it had been nothing but her iron will that had brought her back from Death's door, and Alastair knew he could not allow her to go there again.

It was a battle she had to fight on her own.

All he could do was hold her hand, and Alastair knew he could not do so again.

Losing Rory had robbed him of all his strength. He was no longer the man he had once been.

His muscles tensed as he pushed Connor's hands off his shoulders. "She'll be better off without me. Perhaps another can see her happy." Then he turned and walked away, knowing that the day Deidre gave her heart to another would be the day his own would stop beating.

Chapter Three

FOR THE LOVE OF A CHILD

Walking down the wide corridor leading to the great hall, Deidre heard the echo of happy voices, mothers, fathers and their children. Laughter and joy danced through the air, whispering of a jolly Yuletide season shared with family, with loved ones. Always had Deidre loved the cold season, the warmth of the roaring fire in the hearth, the way everyone huddled together, cheeks flushed and eyes glowing.

With a sigh, she stopped in the arched doorway, standing back so that those in the great hall would not see her. Her gaze shifted over Henrietta and Beth sitting near the fireplace, little Dane asleep on the settee beside his mother, before it moved to Connor and Tristan, balancing Bridget and Ellen on their shoulders as they stretched out their little arms to fasten red ribbons and straw stars to the evergreen garlands and boughs hung around the hall. Little Aileen stood a little forlorn beside them, her deep green eyes wide as she watched the proceedings, a hint of longing on her face.

"Mummy, look how pretty!" Ellen called from up on her father's shoulders as she leaned sideways to point at a red ribbon she had just tied to a branch.

As her balance shifted, Tristan stumbled to the side to keep them from tumbling over. "Would you sit still?" he growled, his hands grasping his daughter's legs. "Or we shall trade places!"

Connor's booming laugh echoed through the great hall. "I wouldna recommend that. Yer little one will snap like kindling."

Sighing, Tristan grinned as his daughter giggled, her eyes shifting to Bridget, who joined in without further prompting.

Leaning against the stone wall, utter longing grew in Deidre's heart as she watched the peaceful scene. If only she could join in! If only she could sit with Henrietta and Beth while Alastair was balancing Rory on his shoulders! If only!

They had been so close to finally having the life they had always dreamed of. So close.

And then it had slipped away in the night, leaving behind nothing but pain and regret.

These days, Deidre no longer knew what to do. Aye, she wanted her husband back, but Alastair seemed determined to keep her at arm's length. Except for the day he had found her by the ruins, he never sought her out. They spent their days separately, only ever crossing each other's path by accident. He rarely spoke to her or even looked at her, his blue eyes cast downward as though he no longer found the strength to care.

At night, he came to their chamber only after he was certain she had fallen asleep, then rose again in the morning before she woke. Only the lingering warmth on his side of the bed whispered of his presence. Deidre often wondered when the day would come that he simply would not return but find another bed to sleep in.

It would be the end of their love, their marriage, and yet, Deidre knew not how to prevent it. Every day, she felt him drifting farther away until one day she knew she would no longer be able to reach him.

Nay, she could not wait. She needed to find a way to him now before it was too late. But how? He still loved her. That, Deidre was sure of. Still, she also knew that he could be as thick-headed as a bull once had made up his mind, and for some reason, he no longer believed that they belonged together. Never would she have thought that Alastair could lose faith in them!

"Now, don't ye fret," Connor chided Bridget as he set her down and picked up little Aileen. "'Tis very unbecoming. Aileen deserves a turn. Now, be a good sister and pass up some of the wee ribbons."

Pouting, Bridget still did as she was told, and before long, all the girls were laughing and giggling once more, pulling on their fathers' hair and almost bringing them to their knees. Oh, if only Rory could be here!

For a long while, Deidre simply stood in the doorway, unable to move into the hall as though somehow, she did not belong, as though she had no right to join in. Still, watching them all so happy warmed her heart, and she was not certain if she felt happy or sad. Perhaps a bit of both. Perhaps she could no longer find true happiness. Perhaps now that they had lost Rory, happiness would always come with a bit of sadness.

Perhaps it was right to be so.

Footsteps echoed closer from behind her, and Deidre heard children's voices travelling down the corridor toward her. She glanced over her shoulder and saw seven-year-old Tillie and her cousin Jonathan race around the corner. The two-year-old boy tripped over his own feet as he tried to keep up with her and fell forward, his nose connecting painfully with the hard-stone floor.

A jolt went through Deidre at his wail, and without thought, she rushed toward him, pulling him into her arms and mumbling words of comfort.

"What happened?"

Looking up, Deidre found Beth's half-sister Adelaide standing there, eyes wide, before she knelt beside them. Reluctantly, Deidre handed the boy to his mother. "He slipped and fell, but I dunna think 'tis so bad."

Tillie peeked at his little face. "He's not even bleeding," she observed wisely.

Adelaide chuckled, gently rocking her little son. "Ah, if only it were that simple," she told Tillie with a pointed glance. "The wounds one cannot see are often the worst ones."

Deidre looked at the young woman, wondering what pain lived in her past that had brought her to that realisation.

Her raven-black hair framed gentle features, and her blue eyes held something wistful as she looked at her little niece. The girl bore a striking resemblance to her; Tillie's eyes, however, still held the usual glow of innocence, free from the darkness the world often forced on one later in life.

"Beth asked us to join them in the great hall," Adelaide told Deidre with a grateful smile, "but I'm afraid we've gotten a little lost."

Deidre smiled. "Aye, 'tis a vast castle." She winked at Tillie. "But the girls love to go exploring all its nooks and crannies. I'm certain Bridget and Ellen would love for you to join them. Right now, they're in the great hall," she pointed down the corridor, "putting up decorations."

Tillie's eyes grew wide with joy. "I love decorations," she exclaimed and then dashed off.

Adelaide smiled as Jonathan looked after his cousin, his eyes drying. "Me go, too," he said pointing, his wide blue eyes turning to his mother.

"Why are we all standing in the hallway?" Adelaide's husband Matthew asked as he and his brother-in-law John came walking around the corner. He pinched his son's cheek before sweeping him into his arms. Then he slung an arm around his wife and together they walked down the hallway and into the great hall.

Beside her, John sighed, his head moving from side to side. "They're nauseatingly happy, are they not?"

Deidre smiled, her gaze shifting from the happy family to the man standing next to her. "Don't we all long for this kind of happiness?"

Running a hand through his dark hair, John shrugged, his features tense as he drew in a deep breath as though uncertain how to answer. Then his blue eyes turned to her, a hint of pain there that she would not have expected. "We all long for something," he whispered as he moved forward.

Deidre followed, surprised when he stopped in the arched doorway where she had already spent the past half hour.

His gaze travelled over the families gathered there, their happy faces turned to one another, and she could not shake the feeling that the man beside her knew well the absence of happiness. Of course, they had only been introduced a few days ago. However, Deidre knew the meaning of pain and regret. She knew what it looked like, and she knew how to see it in those around her.

"Is it Tillie's mother?" she whispered, wondering if it would help him to speak about whatever it was that rested so heavily on his heart.

His eyes closed, and he rubbed a hand over his face. "I'm her father in name only," he finally said, his gaze drifting to the little black-haired girl, her nimble fingers working a long straw into a little star. "Adelaide has always taken care of her. I'm no good with children."

Deidre frowned, wondering about this odd way of replying to her question. She would have expected him to say that he did not wish to speak of Tillie's mother. However, the way he moved the conversation to himself made her wonder even more what had happened in his past; a past he clearly regretted.

The men rose and reached for their winter coats, Henrietta joining them as they all headed for the door. "They'll head out to cut the Yule log," Deidre told him. "Would ye like to accompany them?"

John shook his head and remained where he was. "I'd rather not."

After the door had closed behind the small group, Beth and Adelaide moved over to the small table where the girls continued to tie small ribbons and fashion stars out of straw. Jonathan and Dane, who had awakened when the men had bustled out the door, laughing and shouting with anticipation, sat on the rug playing with wooden animals.

"Where is Miss Harmon? Sophie?" Deidre asked, wondering what could be on John's mind as he stood staring at his little daughter. "I haven't seen her in the past two days. I hope she is well."

"Adelaide said it was a minor stomach affliction," John replied, his gaze never drifting to her. "She told her to remain in bed and rest."

Deidre nodded, wondering what to do. A part of her did not feel right leaving John on his own when there was clearly something troubling him.

While Ellen and Bridget soon lost interest and disappeared on another exploration of the castle, little Aileen trailing in their wake, Tillie remained, her head bent over her work.

"She loves to paint," John mumbled, a faraway look in his eyes. "I don't see her that often these days now that she lives with Adelaide and Matthew. But when I come to visit, she always hands me a new painting." A soft smile tugged on his lips. "I don't know what to do with them."

"Ye love her dearly, do ye not?" Deidre whispered, wondering about the conflict she glimpsed in John's demeanour. He clearly loved the girl; yet, the way he looked at her spoke of sadness as though he had no right to.

He drew in a long breath, "Yes, I love her. She's my...she's my daughter after all."

Deidre frowned. "Is she?"

What had prompted her to ask this, Deidre could not say; however, the way John's head whipped around, his eyes wide and staring at her in utter panic, she had not expected, not seen it coming. His pulse pounded in his neck, and he turned pale as though ready to faint.

For a long moment, they simply looked at one another, both lost for words, both needing time to accept the revelation of the past minutes. "I willna say a word," Deidre assured him, reading deepest concern in his eyes. "Ye needna worry. I promise."

John swallowed hard. Then he nodded. "Thank you." His hands clenched at his sides. "How did you know?"

Deidre shrugged. "That I canna say." Again, her gaze drifted to Tillie as Adelaide came to sit beside her, her hands reaching out to help the girl tie a smaller ribbon. They smiled at each other, their blue eyes full of affection. "She's Adelaide's, is she not?" Deidre whispered, her voice barely audible.

Out of the corner of her eye, she saw John's jaw tense before he turned to look at her, his gaze uncertain as he sought hers. Then his eyes closed, and he nodded, the movement almost imperceptible. Still, it seemed as though a heavy burden slid off his shoulders in that moment, and Deidre knew that he had been carrying this secret with him ever since Tillie had been born.

"D'ye wish to talk about it?" she asked gently.

A muscle in his jaw twitched. "I mustn't," was all he said, and yet, she could see that he desperately needed to.

Chapter Four

A WOMAN'S CHOICE

T he march through the snow had felt good, and Alastair welcomed the heaviness that fell over his limbs. The cold stung his face; yet, his heart beat fast, warming his body and giving him strength. It had been a while since he had felt this alive.

At least in body if not in heart and soul.

However, the moment they carried the Yule log into the great hall, something cold gripped his heart and squeezed tightly as though wishing to bring him to his knees. He almost lost his step as his gaze was drawn to his wife, seated with the others in front of the warm fire, her soft brown eyes lingering on Beth's half-brother as he read to his young daughter.

Gritting his teeth, Alastair forced his gaze away, willing himself to concentrate on the conversation between the men, on settling the Yule log in a corner of the room awaiting the Yuletide feast, on the cheering children who ran to their sides as they came through the door, treading snow into the hall.

Still, nothing held his attention for long, and as the evening wore on, he found his gaze straying to her again and again. Usually, he would have left; however, something dark simmered in his blood, something primal and possessive, and Alastair did not dare abandon her side.

Instead, he watched her, watched her gaze linger on the English-man, watched the man's eyes rise and meet hers, a soft smile coming to his lips, matching her own. He saw warmth there and closeness, the first sparks of depth and intimacy as though they had known each other far longer than a mere few days.

"Ye look ready to murder someone," Connor observed as he came to stand beside him in a far corner of the hall. "Pray tell, what has our guest done to ye?"

"'Tis nothing!" Alastair hissed, his arms feeling ready to break as he clenched them in front of his chest.

Connor laughed, "Aye, 'tis nothing." He shook his head. "If ye want anyone to believe that, then ye need to stop glowering at the poor man."

Alastair's teeth ground together painfully as he fought to remain in control, well-aware that his cousin was baiting him.

"Without a wife, I suppose he feels a bit lonely over the holidays," Connor continued, leaning his back against the wall beside Alastair, watching him out of the corner of his eye. "I havena had the chance to speak to him much, but he strikes me as a decent man. Henrietta told me that Beth and Adelaide are hoping he'll find a wife soon. After all, he's a good catch. He's inherited his father's title a few years back and has been working hard to get the estate back up onto its feet. He'll be more than able to provide for a-"

Alastair spun to glare at his cousin. "Then he ought to look else-where and keep his eyes off *my wife!*"

A slow grin spread over Connor's face. "Perhaps ye ought to tell him that." He glanced at Deidre. "And her as well. I'm certain she would love to hear it."

Huffing out a breath through gritted teeth, Alastair rested the back of his head against the wall, closing his eyes. His emotions ran rampant, and he knew not how to leash them back in. He knew what he ought to do, and yet, he could not bring himself to move.

To step aside.

To grant her this chance for happiness.

"Ye love her still," Connor said gently, his large hand settling on Alastair's shoulder, "and she loves ye. Dunna be a fool and-"

"Oh, does she?" Alastair snapped, knowing that he was not being fair. Still, the way Deidre kept looking at the Englishman turned his stomach and pierced his heart. "To me, it seems she's already moved on." His muscles were so tense, they felt ready to snap at any moment. "She's wise to do so," he gritted out, the words like ashes in his mouth.

Connor heaved an exasperated sigh, "Ye canna know what happened," he counselled. "Aye, I agree they seem...close," a dark growl rose from Alastair's throat, "for two people who've only just met, but ye dunna know why. Perhaps they simply found...common ground."

Alastair scoffed.

"Aye, we dunna know what happened to the girl's mother, and Deidre-"

"Lost more than anyone ever should," Alastair finished for his cousin, his mind reasoning that perhaps the Englishman could comfort Deidre where Alastair had left her alone. She was only right to seek solace elsewhere after he had denied her his own. She was only doing what he had told her to do.

He had told her they were not meant for each other.

He had told her that perhaps the man she would meet up by the ruins would be better for her.

He had told her all that and more, not with words but with the way he had been treating her.

Deidre deserved better. She deserved a man who would stand with her, hold her, comfort her, offer her his strength.

And Alastair could no longer be that man.

Still, the thought that Deidre would give her heart to another, perhaps even the Englishman sitting right here under his roof, nearly brought him to his knees. Perhaps he ought to leave after all. Perhaps then the strain would lessen.

Alastair doubted it very much.

"I canna watch this any longer," he grumbled, forcing his feet to turn away. Then he marched off down a dark hallway, his thoughts elsewhere as his legs carried him through the castle. Oddly enough, he soon found himself in front of their chamber, the place they had shared ever since they had been married so many years ago.

Memories tugged on his heart, and he pushed open the door.

Stepping inside the large chamber, Alastair allowed his gaze to linger here and there as memories surfaced, memories of times untainted by pain and loss. Unable not to, he closed the door behind him and moved farther into the room, striding across the warm rug in front of the fireplace as his eyes glided from the bed, to the armchairs and back. Here, they had lived together, only the two of them. They had laughed and cried, fought and argued and reconciled. They had read to one another, gazed into the fire together and listened to the rain as it drummed on the windowpanes.

Here, they had been happy together.

They had been Deidre and Alastair.

They had been meant to be.

Always.

But no more. Could he truly let her go? Was he strong enough to set her free?

Hanging his head, Alastair felt the cool glass of the window as his forehead settled against it. It was oddly soothing, and yet, whispered of a cold future without the woman he loved by his side and in his arms.

For how long he simply stood there, forehead resting against the cool glass, Alastair did not know. His thoughts turned to the past, to happier times, and he allowed himself a small reprieve, a moment of pretence in which all was well and forever would be.

And then the door creaked open behind him, and the soft scent of roses drifted to his nose.

Alastair closed his eyes, realising his mistake. Aye, he was still angry with her, with that *Englishman*, with the world. He wanted to rant and scream and run his fist through the wall, feel the stone crumble under his anger. He wanted to stand tall, to meet her gaze with a defiant one of his own. He wanted to shake her, to lash out at her.

But even more than that, he wanted to pull her into his arms and hold her close. He wanted to bury his face in her hair and breathe in the soft scent of her. He wanted to feel her hands brushing over his back, soothing and comforting as they had countless times before. He wanted those deep brown eyes to look into his and know with a single glance the depth of his despair, his longing. He wanted his wife back.

And it took every ounce of strength Alastair could find to maintain the hard edge in his gaze as he turned to look at her.

With her soft brown curls framing her gentle face, Deidre stood in the doorway, a hint of disbelief in her soulful eyes as though she could not quite believe what she was seeing.

Truth be told, Alastair had begun to avoid his wife in recent months, unable to bear the burden of being near her and keeping her at arm's length at the same time. It was easier to simply avoid her altogether. He could not even remember the last time he had returned to their chamber before she had fallen asleep.

"I'm surprised to see ye," she whispered as though afraid to chase him away. A small smile touched her lips as she reached back to close the door. "But I'm glad."

Alastair felt his muscles tense, fighting to keep him where he was, to keep him from reaching for her. "Are ye?" he growled, tapping into his anger instead of his longing for her. It was by far the safer option. "Ye seemed quite content in the hall."

Her gaze narrowed ever so slightly, a hint of confusion coming to her dark eyes. "'Tis nice to have guests, is it not? Especially during the cold season when one is confined indoors." She took a step toward him.

Alastair tensed. "Ye seemed to be enjoying the company of a particular *gentleman*." The moment the words left his lips, he knew them to be a mistake. Had he not reasoned that it would be best for both if he set her free? If he gave her his blessing to move on? To seek happiness?

Her brows drew down, and still she moved closer, her gaze lingering on his face, seeing all he could not say. "Ye speak about John?"

Alastair's jaw clenched, and for a moment, he feared his teeth would crack under the pressure. Still, to hear her call *that man* by his given name brought a pain to Alastair's heart he knew only too well. "Ye seem to have grown close in only a few days."

Something sparked in her eyes, and the right corner of her mouth twitched. "He's a nice man, and I admit I enjoy his company."

Alastair's hands balled into fists, and he hid them behind his back. "I hear he's looking for a wife." Physical pain began to surge through his body; still, he fought to stay the course.

The soft smile on his wife's face deepened. "Any woman would be happy to call him husband." Again, the corner of her mouth twitched.

Alastair groaned. His insides twisted and turned painfully even though he knew she was taunting him. He could see it in her eyes, that hint of expectation, of anticipation. She wanted him to lose the battle waging within him. She wanted him to break the shackles he had forced on himself.

He exhaled a deep breath. She wanted him. He knew that. He could see it in her eyes, and he felt his heart respond, urging him to drop this mask of anger and detachment, and seize her right here and now.

Still, he restrained himself, and a part of him felt as though he would go mad with the tension that held him in an iron vice. "What did Moira write in her letter?" he asked, needing to distract her, to distract himself.

Deidre's smile faltered. "Moira?" She swallowed before inhaling a long breath, full of disappointment. "I already told ye, did I not? Why would ye ask me again?"

"What *exactly* did she write?" Alastair pressed, needing to be certain that his sacrifice would lead to happiness for his wife.

With a sigh, Moira turned toward the armoire in the corner and dove into one of the drawers. A moment later, she held an envelope in her hand. "Read for yerself," she said, holding it out to him.

Unclenching his hand, Alastair stepped forward to receive the item that was to determine their future. His fingers felt the smooth texture of the paper before their tips brushed against Deidre's warm skin.

Alastair all but jerked the envelope from her hand, his own still tingling with the short contact. He swallowed as his eyes held hers for a moment longer, still amazed after all these years how deeply she affected him.

Then his gaze dropped to the parchment, and his insides twisted and turned once more as he read his sister's words. As he had feared-or hoped? -there was no certainty in her prediction, only the idea of something that *might* come to pass.

· · ·

All I can tell you is that on the day marked by the blue flower, you're to seek out the old ruins, and there you will stumble upon a great love.

Alastair closed his eyes, remembering the many times over the past year his wife had gone for a ride. He knew she had needed time and space to mourn their daughter, to find a way to continue. And he had understood.

But had her rides been more than the desire for solitude? Had she been looking for something else?

"Ye've sought out the ruins often, have ye not?" Alastair asked, his gaze seeking hers once more. "Ye believe what Moira wrote. Ye believe it'll come to pass, and ye're waiting for," his jaw clenched, "the man ye can give yer heart to."

As he spoke, her eyes widened as understanding slowly found her. Then, however, her gaze narrowed, and he could see a touch of anger curling at the corners of her mouth. "Do ye truly believe that?" she demanded, hands on her hips and fury in her eyes. "Do ye truly mean to say that my love for ye is as fleeting as a summer's breeze?" Disappointment swirled in her brown eyes as she stared at him. "Is that what ye think?"

Alastair pulled back his shoulders and hardened his heart. "It doesna matter what I think." He swallowed. "Few things last forever, and perhaps this is a sign that we should never have been. That there is a new chance for ye to find happiness." He inhaled an agonisingly deep breath. "With someone other than me."

Shaking her head, Deidre stared at him. "But we're married," she stated, her voice once more gaining strength. "I am *yer* wife, and ye are *my* husband. There can never be another."

Alastair fought the warmth her words conjured. "Perhaps not another husband, but another love."

Her mouth clamped shut, and anger blazed to life in her eyes.

Alastair loved her for it. "Ye need to be reasonable," he said, forcing each word from his lips. "We're not meant for each other. We never were. Ye canna deny that. Not now. Not after..." His voice trailed off, unable to speak his daughter's name out loud.

The look in Deidre's gaze softened, and she began to move toward him.

Alastair flinched, halting her in her step. "Perhaps there's truly a higher power," he pushed on, needing to say this before his determination crumbled into dust. "Perhaps there's a different plan for us. Perhaps we ought to have listened to my parents." He swallowed hard. "Not for my sake, but for yers. Ye canna deny that-"

His voice broke off as she strode toward him, her lips pressed into a thin line and tears misting her eyes. Her cheeks had reddened with the depth of emotions bubbling in her blood, and the moment she drew near, her right hand pulled back and she slapped him hard across the cheek. "Dunna ever say that!" she snapped between sobs. "Ye married me because ye loved me. Have ye forgotten that?"

Blinking back tears, Alastair fought the urge to reach for her, the sting in his cheek only a minor discomfort compared to the way his heart broke in two at the sight of her desperate fury. "I havena forgotten. But perhaps 'twas not enough."

"'Twas enough for me!" she told him, adamant in the way she stood before him, her dark brown eyes unwavering, not bearing the slightest hint of doubt or uncertainty. "'Tis enough for me." She blinked, and a lone tear snaked down her cheek. "But not for ye? Are ye trying to tell me that ye dunna feel for me any longer? That yer heart is mine no more? That ye long for another?"

The absurdity of her words struck him hard in the chest. "All I meant to say is that the path we chose was not the one meant for us. Perhaps we-"

"I dunna care!" His delicate, little wife all but screamed into his face. "I dunna believe in *meant-to-be*. I dunna believe in fate or destiny. I dunna believe in a higher power. I dunna believe ye were meant for me." She inhaled a deep breath, her chest rising and falling with the agitation burning in her blood. "Perhaps I did once, but no more."

Even though her words only confirmed what Alastair himself had reasoned, he could not deny the pain it brought to hear her speak them. "Then we're agreed."

Deidre scoffed, "We're far from agreed." With her eyes on his, she moved closer, her dainty feet closing the remaining distance between them until she stood all but pressed against him, her hands on his chest, her fingers curled into his shirt.

Her gentle eyes burnt hard as they held his, daring him to contradict her, threatening retribution should he be foolish enough to do so. "I no longer believe things are meant to be. There's good and there's bad in the world. There's pain and there's joy. We canna feel one without the other, but I dunna believe that all that comes to pass was meant to happen." Her hands tensed, and he felt himself pulled toward her, her eyes burning into his. "I *chose* ye."

Those three words spoken with such conviction, such belief, without even the slightest room for doubt or error, slid down his spine, sending shivers over his skin. Her breath fanned over his lips, and he felt his own coming faster as he stared down into her eyes.

"I *chose* ye," she repeated as her hands flattened against his chest, then slid higher. "And ye chose me. We did so not because 'twas part of someone's plan, but out of our own free will." Her hands snaked around his neck, pulling him down to her, her lips barely a hair's breadth away from his. "I chose ye, and I would do so again in a heartbeat." Her lips brushed against his in a feather-light touch before her brown eyes once more found his. "Would ye?"

Chapter Five

SHARED SORROW

Clinging to her husband, Deidre fought the despair that clawed at her heart.

Something in his eyes whispered of more than a broken heart, but a soul in peril. The wound was deep and refused to heal, cut open yet again every time he pushed her away. Every time he refused her offer of comfort. Every time he forced himself not to feel.

His muscles trembled with the effort it took him to remain standing, to keep his hands behind his back, to keep from reaching for her. His jaw clenched shut as he stared down into her eyes, temptation and longing swirling in their depths, held at bay by the very stubbornness that had always endeared him to her. Only now, it kept them apart. It kept him locked in this battle, day in and out.

Alone.

Perhaps before Alastair could accept her help, her comfort, he first needed to break completely. Perhaps he had not yet reached that point where nothing mattered but one's next breath. The point where there was no shame, no guilt, no duty, but only truth, free and unrestrained.

Deidre knew that it would bring him pain, but she was desperate, and so she reached for the one thing she knew had the power to break him. With her hands on his chest, his heart beating fast against her palms, she held his gaze. "I know ye carry a lock of her hair."

For a split second, her husband froze, shock marking his features, before he jerked away from her as though she had slapped him. As unyielding and strong as he had been all his life, Alastair Brunwood could not seem to bring himself to fight through the pain of his daughter's loss and chose to flee it instead.

However, Deidre was ready for it. Her fingers curled into his shirt and held on, not allowing him to run. She could see an almost desperate plea in his eyes as tears began to pool in their corners, and her heart ached, willing her fingers to loosen, to grant him the reprieve he so desperately needed.

But she did not. She held on, her eyes fixed on his, daring him to confide in her, promising to catch him should he crumble under the weight of his pain.

Again, he jerked away, and when her hands would not release him, his settled around her wrists, trying to free himself of her hold. They were cold and hard, matching the dull ache in his gaze. Still, she felt his pulse hammering in his veins and remembered the warmth that had always lived in his heart.

"I willna release ye," she whispered, her fingers curling tighter into the fabric of his shirt. "I willna allow ye to run from this all yer life."

A growl rumbled in his chest. "I'm not-"

"Aye, ye are!" She shook him. "Ye are! And I willna have it!"

His breath came fast as he stared at her, his jaw still clenched; and yet, Deidre could see a small crack in his armour. His shoulders slumped ever so slightly, and for the length of a heartbeat or two, he closed his eyes, a deep breath shuddering past his lips.

"Say her name."

At her whispered words, his eyes flew open in shock, and his hands tensed on her wrists like iron shackles. The need to flee once more blazed in his eyes, and Deidre tightened her hold on him instinctively.

"Say her name."

Once more, Alastair tried to yank himself free of her hold, but Deidre clung to him, her eyes seeking his again and again as he dropped his gaze, as he looked past her, as he fought not to see her right there in front of him, alive and warm and strong, willing him to live.

"Say her name."

His jaw began to tremble, and a tear rolled down his cheek as his hands slid from her wrists and down along her arms. Like a tree cut down, he slowly sank forward as his last line of defence began to fall.

And then his arms were around her, his forehead resting against her shoulder, his warm breath tickling the sensitive skin on her neck as he held her clutched in his embrace.

Deidre felt tears stream down her face as she held him, her arms rising to wrap around him, brushing gently over his broad back. "Say her name," she whispered yet again, needing him to surrender. It would pain him, break him, but only then would he have a chance to heal. "Please," she whispered, her lips brushing against his ear. "I promise I'll catch ye when ye fall as ye've always caught me. Ye've always been my strength, now let me be yers. I swear I willna crumble under the weight of it. Ye needna be afraid. Please."

Another breath shuddered past his lips as a tremor shook him, and she could feel the wetness of his tears on her skin. "Rory."

The sound of their daughter's name on his lips was barely a whisper, and yet, Deidre felt it in every fibre of her being. Her heart clenched in pain and jumped with joy at the sound of it.

It was beautiful.

It was heart-breaking.

It was theirs.

Theirs alone.

As though all strength had left him, Alastair's knees suddenly buckled. Unable to hold him, Deidre gave in, and they both sank to the floor, arms wrapped around each other, mourning the loss of their child.

Together.

As they ought to have from the beginning.

Back then, Alastair had held her as well. He had let her cry. He' had been her comfort, her rock, her strength. But he had not accepted the same from her. He had not shown her his own wound, his pain and sorrow, and over time, the wound had begun to fester, digging deeper into his flesh.

"She was such a sweet lass," Deidre whispered into his ear, remembering the awe she had felt when she had held her daughter for the first time. "Always smiling. Her eyes wide and watchful. The whole world a wonder to her."

With each word she spoke, Deidre felt the walls around her husband's heart crumble bit by bit. He pulled her deeper into his embrace, clinging to her as pain and loss washed over him. Tears now streamed freely from his eyes, soaking her dress as he kept his face buried in the crook of her neck.

"She was always so warm," Deidre remembered, "and I loved holding her snuggled against me. She fit perfectly into my arms, and I often sat in that chair over there," she nodded her head at the armchair by the hearth, "and watched her sleep, her little eyes closed, her wee lashes resting gently against her rosy skin." A sob wrenched itself from her throat. "She was so beautiful."

Alastair's left hand moved from her back and up her arm until his hand cupped her face, his thumb gently brushing the tears from her cheek. Still, he did not lift his head to look at her, and Deidre knew that the pain was still too raw. At least, he was not pushing her away as he had before.

"When she was born," Deidre went on, her fingers curling into her husband's hair, "I couldna believe the scarlet curls on top of her head. I thought 'twas a trick of light. They made her look so mischievous." More tears flowed from her eyes, and yet, a small smile played on her lips. "One corner of her wee mouth curled upward, and I had to laugh. She had such a devilish look about her."

Alastair's lips brushed against her skin as he placed a gentle kiss on her neck. Then his head slowly rose off her shoulder, his blue eyes rising to meet hers. Tears still lingered, but he no longer tried to hide them. Instead, his gaze met hers with an openness she had not seen in a long time. He inhaled a deep breath before his eyes fell from hers and his hand dug into his pocket.

Deidre swallowed, certain beyond the shadow of a doubt what he was about.

A moment later, she found herself looking at her daughter's fiery-red curl, a soft blue ribbon tied around it. It looked dwarfed lying on his big hand, the same way, Rory had always seemed when cuddled in her father's large arms.

His eyes caressed the tiny curl lovingly before they rose and met hers. He blinked as fresh tears shot to his eyes, and his lips pressed into a tight line, the corners of his mouth quivering under the rush of emotions the memory of their daughter had brought forth.

Deidre nodded, reaching out a hand to cup his face. She knew her husband. She knew that he was not a man of many words, and she did not mind. She could see how deeply he cared. She did not need him to say the words. What she wanted was for him to share these moments with her, the good as well as the bad.

Especially the bad.

With one hand cradling her husband's face, Deidre reached out with the other and once more closed his fingers over Rory's soft curl. "We'll always remember her," she whispered, her eyes searching his. "Together."

Nodding, Alastair reached for her, pulling her onto his lap, his large arms all but pinning her to him as his lips claimed hers in a gentle kiss. "I love ye, my wee wife," he whispered as he had so often before.

Deidre smiled against his lips, and for the first time in almost two years, hope blossomed in her heart. "Will ye hold me tonight?" she asked, her gaze seeking his. A part of her still feared that he would retreat once more, urging her to reclaim him now before he could change his mind.

Before he could rebuild the walls that had come down.

His blue eyes met hers, held hers for a long while, before he moved closer, his lips once more capturing hers. "Aye, I'll hold ye." He swallowed. "If ye'll hold me."

Smiling, Deidre nodded, her heart dancing with joy at the longing in his voice. With one hand holding on to his, she climbed off his lap, then helped pull him to his feet. All the while, their hands remained linked as though they could not exist without the touch of the other.

Her heart beat fast as she pulled her husband toward the bed; the bed they had not truly shared since the loss of their child. Alastair

BREE WOLF

swallowed as his gaze travelled over the two sides, two halves of a whole. Two halves that had been separated for too long.

His chest rose and fell with a deep breath as he gently settled their daughter's scarlet lock on the nightstand. Then he turned to her, one arm coming around her middle, pulling her against his side, while the other reached to pull down the blanket.

Although Deidre's heart beat almost nervously in her chest, she revelled in the warmth that claimed her at the closeness which once more spanned the distance between them. Once, it had connected them even across miles and miles of distance. Perhaps, it could do so again.

Now, however, it seemed important that they touch, that he had his hand on her back as she climbed into bed, that her hand reach for him, sliding up his arm, as he followed.

Settling into the soft mattress, Alastair pulled her to him, her head coming to rest on his shoulder as she snuggled closer. His hand brushed up her arm, then gently squeezed her shoulder before she felt the tips of his fingers running through her hair, brushing a curl behind her ear.

Her own hand moved over his chest, the tips of her fingers finding the collar and then warm skin. Reaching up, she brushed her hand along the soft skin in the crook between shoulder and neck, feeling the rapid drumming of his pulse. She dragged her fingernails up and down the side of his neck, her thumb tracing the line of his jaw.

A low rumble in his throat whispered of his contentedness, and a moment later, he pulled her deeper into his embrace, both arms holding her tightly against him. His legs tangled with hers, and Deidre sighed at the feeling of closeness and intimacy that warmed her. Always had they existed as one, and in the past two years, life had been cold and lonely.

Deidre did not want to feel cold and lonely any longer. She wanted warmth and love and...her husband in her arms.

On impulse, she lifted her head and kissed the side of his neck where his pulse beat steadily, contentedly as her own.

At the touch of her lips, Alastair paused, and the hand that trailed circles across her arm stilled. A few harsh breaths pushed past his lips

44

before he suddenly moved, rolling over and trapping her beneath him, answering her silent call.

All restraint fell from him, and his lips claimed hers in a searing kiss. Longing and passion flared to life, reminders of what they had once shared, a promise of what they could have again.

Her hands moved back to encircle his neck, her fingertips trailing under his shirt, as her husband shifted to undo the laces on her dress. Soon, skin touched skin as they reached for one another in the dark of night, the few glowing embers in the hearth casting a warm light over their reunion.

Meant to be or not, Deidre would never let him go again.

Damn his stubbornness! If she had to, she would do him one better!

Chapter Six

IN THE BRIGHT OF DAY

Pulling the cloak tighter around her shoulders, Deidre walked across the great hall of Greystone Castle. She cast a smile at Henrietta and their guests as they sat together by the hearth, the wee ones chasing each other around the large stone columns and down the wide corridors before they came rushing back, seeking refuge in their mothers' arms.

"Are ye heading out?" Connor spoke out from behind her.

Turning to look at her cousin, Deidre nodded. "Aye, I need a bit of fresh air." She pushed open the heavy door, inhaling a deep breath of the clear, chilled air. The snow had stopped falling, and her gaze drifted over the white courtyard, the black cobble stones hidden under a thick layer of snow. The sky shone in a clear blue, and the sun sent out tentative rays that sparkled on the ice-covered rooves.

"Have ye spoken to Alastair since yesterday?" Connor enquired as he came to stand beside her. His dark gaze lingered on her face, and she could see that there was something on his mind, his forehead creased with lines of worry.

Deidre swallowed, not certain whether to reveal all that had happened the night before for she could not yet say where it would lead. Aye, Alastair had responded to her, had shared his grief with her, had given in to his own longing for what they had once had. But he had risen early that morning, leaving their bed without waking her.

Had doubts returned?

Of course, they had, for Alastair was a man who rarely did anything on impulse. He was ruled by his mind, not by his heart, and always had been.

Except when it came to her.

Against all reason, Alastair had chosen her all those years ago, and Deidre knew that wherever she was concerned, he often acted rashly and without thought. She was his weakness, always had been, and she could only hope that that had not changed. That he merely needed a moment to himself, that he needed to think things through as was his way, and that he would then realise that he could not fight what his heart desired.

"Have ye seen him this morning?" Deidre asked, wondering where her husband could have gone.

Connor nodded, and his gaze travelled to the far hills. "He left early." He sighed, then turned to meet her eyes. "There was an odd look in his eyes. Haunted somehow, but..." His voice trailed off, and then he shrugged. "I canna say. It doesna make me worry, but...wonder."

Deidre nodded. "I shall speak to him when he returns." Her gaze caught movement in the far corner of the courtyard where the tall hedge stood that hid her sanctuary from the rest of the world. A man lingered nearby before he moved closer, his hands pushing aside a few branches, revealing the secret path. "He found it," she mumbled, feeling a touch of annoyance that someone had stumbled upon her sanctuary.

Connor moved a step sideways, his gaze following her own. "'Tis John, aye?" he asked squinting his eyes against the early morning sun. Then a chuckle rumbled in his throat. "'Twould seem yer secret hideout is no longer a secret."

Deidre shook her head at her bear-like cousin. "I dunna mind sharing," she told him, willing it to be so. "'Tis only that no one's shown an interest in the place for a long time."

Connor winked at her. "'Twould seem someone is now." A good-

47

natured smile lingered on his face until Deidre made to step away, her feet guiding her in the direction of her secret garden. "Wait, Lassie!" His hand settled on her shoulder as she turned back to look at him. "I know I'm an oaf for asking ye this, but..." He inhaled a deep breath. "Is there anything between ye and Beth's brother?"

Remembering her husband's seething jealousy from the night before, Deidre chuckled, "Aye, ye're an oaf as is my husband."

A quick grin flashed across Connor's face before his gaze sobered. "He spoke to ye? I told him he was seeing things, but ye know as well as I that the heart doesna always see what is right in front of it. Perhaps ye shouldna seek out John on yer own. 'Twould only confuse Alastair."

"I will do what I deem right," Deidre told her cousin with a pat on his arm. "As I always have." Her gaze drifted back to the hidden path between hedge and wall where John had disappeared, wondering why he sought solitude when everyone else was laughing and chatting inside.

Very few people needed true solitude. Most needed someone who saw their pain and offered a kind ear. Perhaps she ought to try and speak to him again. Perhaps by now the shock that she had guessed his secret had dissipated.

Casting a smile at her cousin, Deidre headed down the stairs and across the courtyard until she reached the evergreen hedge. She reached out to push aside a few branches and then squeezed through. Still, wetness caught on the front of her dress and she felt droplets trickling down the side of her face.

Stepping into her small sanctuary, Deidre found John standing under one of her apple trees, its branches now barren in the deep of winter. His shoulders seemed slumped, and she could all but see the weight resting upon them. "I see ye've found my little garden," she greeted him as she moved forward across the snow-covered ground.

At the sound of her voice, his head snapped around; however, when his gaze fell upon her, she thought to see a touch of relief. Perhaps he truly needed someone to speak to. A stranger. Someone he did not know. Someone who would simply listen. Someone he need not be afraid of hurting with the truth. "I apologise for intruding," he said, inclining his head to her, the hint of a smile touching his mouth. "I can leave if you..." His words trailed off as though he wanted her to object and ask him to stay.

Deidre smiled at him. "Tell me about Tillie."

The muscles in his throat worked as he swallowed. Then he nodded, inhaling a deep breath. His gaze became distant as his mind churned, returning to the beginning of his story. "Adelaide was always the obedient daughter, and I the wayward son," he began, his feet carrying him around the small enclosure as his thoughts drifted backwards. "Until the day she needed my help."

"She wasna married at the time?" Deidre asked, wondering about the young woman's past and all that had happened to her.

John shook his head, his teeth gritting together. "A friend of mine... took advantage of her," he turned to meet her gaze, "to pay me back for a slight against him. It was my fault she became his target." He sighed, "She gave birth in secret, and then we had the babe placed on our doorstep as though she had been left by her mother." He swallowed, and the look on his face spoke volumes about the anguish that lived in his heart. "I claimed Tillie as mine so Adelaide could keep her without being forced to marry a man she did not want." Exhaling a long breath, he ran his hands through his hair, then over his face. "I lied to protect them, thinking nothing would change because of it."

Deidre moved closer, seeking his gaze. "Ye're her father, and yet, ye're not," she whispered when he looked up. "'Tis hard on the heart."

John nodded, a hint of relief in his eyes that someone understood. "I was nothing but a rake when I was young." He cast her an apologetic glance. "I followed in my father's footsteps. I did what I wanted, and I didn't think about how it affected others." He sighed, and the young man he had once been disappeared behind the man he had become since. "But then Adelaide married Whitworth, and Father died and..."

He turned, and his blue gaze met hers. "I do not want to be that man any longer. I've tried to change. I've done my best to...set everything right, but..." He shook his head, clearly at a loss. "I cannot tell the truth, and a part of me doesn't even want to." A smile flickered across his face. "I love Tillie. I would never hurt her, but now...now

Whitworth is her father. He's the one who reads to her, who tucks her in at night, who comforts her."

Deidre frowned when his lips moved, but no sound came out as though he did not dare speak what lingered on his mind. "Does yer sister want Tillie to know?"

Again, his head snapped up, and again, she saw that mix of shock and relief in his eyes. "You're very perceptive," John mumbled, a hint of awe in his voice. "How did you know?"

Deidre shrugged. "I saw the way Adelaide looked at her. There was longing there, a mother's need for her child."

John nodded. "She spoke to me a few weeks back, saying that she and Whitworth talked about revealing the truth to Tillie. So only she would know." His hands clenched and unclenched as he stared at her. "Then she would know. Then there would be no reason for her to..."

"But she loves ye," Deidre told him, gently placing a hand on his arm. "Do ye not see that?"

A small smile flashed across his face. "But once she knows-"

"'Twill not change anything," Deidre promised him. "Whether ye're her father or her uncle or anyone else, what matters is that ye're in her life, that ye love her, that ye care for her." She squeezed his arm. "Believe me, love is not a problem. 'Tis people who make it one. Ye're allowed to love her. Dunna ever allow others to tell ye how ye ought to feel."

A deep breath rushed from his lips, and Deidre felt his muscles relax under her hand. Casting her a warm smile, he reached into his pocket and pulled out a small straw flower. "Tillie made it," he whispered, affection swinging in his voice. "She has such nimble fingers and a true eye for detail." Looking up, he met her gaze. "She even coloured it."

As he reached to turn it over, the small flower slipped from his hand. Twirling, it drifted downward until it landed in the soft snow, its coloured side facing upward.

The breath lodged in Deidre's lungs as she stared down at the small, *blue* flower surrounded by the snow's blinding brightness. Her knees buckled, and she clamped a hand on John's arm to steady herself. Moira's vision!

The blue flower!

"Are you all right?" John asked, and she felt his gaze on her face. "You look suddenly pale. Did I say somethi-?"

"No," Deidre assured him as she knelt and gingerly picked up the small item. Her heart beat wildly in her chest, and her head spun with the implications of the moment. Was she to head to the ruins now? And what would she find there? Who would she find there? John? She looked up at him, a frown tugging on her brows. Or was he simply the messenger and this had nothing to do with him?

"Perhaps we should head back inside," John suggested, a touch of unease on his face as he watched her. "Perhaps you need to warm up."

Deidre nodded, unable to catch a clear thought, as they headed back toward the small gap between wall and hedge. "I'm sorry. I feel a little..." She stopped, then turned to look at him. "It has nothing to do with ye, I swear."

John nodded. Still, confusion remained in his eyes. Deidre could only hope her odd behaviour would not lessen the weight of her words.

But what now? Ought she to head to the ruins?

Never in a thousand years would she believe that her heart could ever beat for another. Still, she could not deny that she was curious where Moira's vision would lead.

What should she do?

Chapter Seven

A SISTER'S ADVICE

After returning from a gallop across the snow-covered hills, Alastair brushed down his gelding, feeling the animal's warm flanks and steamy breath after the exertion he had put them both through. His mind and heart were still at war, and yet, the cold, clear air had made him feel more at peace. As though he was now better prepared for whatever lay ahead.

A memory of the previous night drifted into his mind, and he could not deny the smile that claimed his lips at the thought of his wife. Deidre had indeed fought like a lioness, forced him to yield to her, and she had been right to do so.

For the first time in the past two years, Alastair had slept well, his wife in his arms and his daughter's smiling face in his dreams. He had woken to find her arm across his chest, her warm breath fanning over his skin, soft and sweet, and he had not wanted to rise.

Still, he had for he knew that he could not simply surrender to his heart's desire without thought. After all, had he not spent the past few days arguing against a shared future? Had he not concluded that in order to see Deidre happy once more he would need to let her go? Could he simply ignore that and do as he pleased?

Alastair had never been the kind of man to do so. However, in that moment, he wished he was.

His gelding nickered softly, and as Alastair turned his head, brushing a gentle hand over the horse's nose, his gaze noticed that Deidre's white mare was missing. The box was empty. Had she ridden out as well?

A sigh left his lips as he tried to picture the moment she had awakened to find the bed empty and him gone. Had she been angry? Hurt? Or had she understood? If so, then why had she left?

Giving his gelding a final pat, Alastair left the stables and made to cross the courtyard, heading for the great hall. However, his feet stilled when his gaze fell on the secret entrance to his wife's hidden garden. The branches moved as someone pushed through, and Alastair felt his jaw clench when he saw that it was not only Deidre, but also *that Englishman.*

Instantly, he retreated into the shadows of the stables at his back, his gaze narrowed, glued to the two people walking toward the front door. The Englishman bowed his head toward Deidre, his lips moving as he whispered something to her. In answer, Deidre's face rose, and she smiled up at him, her hand coming to rest on his arm, giving it a gentle squeeze.

Although Alastair's mind argued that there could easily be a perfectly reasonable explanation for their behaviour, his heart did not hear a word of it for it was blinded by the fears he had known ever since learning of Moira's vision. Who would be the man who stole Deidre's heart? Could it be this Englishman? Had he already lost her?

After watching them disappear inside, Alastair knew not what to do. Before he had been determined to seek out his wife and...

And what?

Rubbing his hands over his face, Alastair began to pace across the snow-covered courtyard, his gaze again and again drawn to the door leading to the castle's hall. He pictured them together, smiling, eyes gazing at one another, their hands linked, unable to keep apart.

The thought drove Alastair mad, and before he knew it, he was half-way across the courtyard, his feet carrying him onward. He knew he ought to set her free. If *that Englishman* was who she wanted, then he had no right to deny her the happiness she deserved. It did not matter that the thought alone killed him. Still, his feet would not still, pushing him onward until he found himself standing in the great hall, his gaze drifting over smiling faces of friends and family. The little ones were dancing around the Yule log, not yet aflame, their cheerful voices in stark contrast to the darkness in his heart.

His hands balled into fists as his gaze swept the hall, coming up empty. Deidre was nowhere to be found, and neither was that Englishm-

Alastair paused as his eyes spotted him, heading back down the side corridor, which led to the guest quarters.

Again, Alastair found himself in pursuit without a conscious thought. His legs moved of their own accord, carrying him after his rival, his hands still clenched at his sides. Why he needed to speak to that man, Alastair could not say. However, a part of him knew that he could never let her go if he could not be certain that she would be safe.

Safe with that Englishman.

At the sound of his footsteps, angry and determined as they were, Beth's brother paused, then turned to look over his shoulder. The moment he spotted Alastair approaching with hurried steps, his gaze narrowed. "Is something wrong?" he asked, wariness coming to his face as he took note of the anger radiating off Alastair.

Pulling to a stop, Alastair gritted his teeth, linking his hands behind his back lest he do something unwise. "Ye spoke to my wife," he hissed, accusation clear in his voice.

The Englishman's eyes narrowed further, a hint of confusion settling upon his face. "I did."

"Why?" Alastair gritted out.

The man's brows drew down; still, there was a hint of reluctance on his face that made Alastair's blood boil. "She..." He drew in a deep breath, his hands moving, turning a small object from side to side. "She gave me some advice."

That, Alastair had not expected. "Advice?" he asked, willing his anger to subside so his mind could overrule the reckless emotions in his heart. "What about?"

The man's lips thinned. "A personal matter." His throat worked as he swallowed. "It is not something I speak about."

Alastair's gaze narrowed. "Then why did ye tell my wife?"

A small chuckle left the man's lips. "I didn't," he objected, shaking his head as though in disbelief. "She...she simply knew. I don't know how." He shrugged. "Somehow she could see it, I suppose."

Alastair nodded. Aye, Deidre did possess the unnerving ability to see into another's heart. Only the night before she had pushed and prodded until she had broken through his defences, knowing better than he had himself that he was hurting. She had seen it and felt compelled to help. Had she seen pain in that Englishman as well? Had she felt compelled to help? Had that been the reason for the whispered words exchanged between them?

The thought was not only reasonable, but it also soothed the pain radiating throughout his body.

"Nothing untoward happened," the Englishman said, sincerity in his gaze as he looked at Alastair. "Your wife is a wonderful woman, full of kindness and insight, and I shall forever be grateful to her for her keen eyes and compassionate heart. That is all."

A moment ticked by as Alastair weighed the man's words, the truth in them, before he nodded. "That she is."

The Englishman smiled in relief. "You're a fortunate man. I hope one day I'll be equally fortunate to find such a woman to love."

Again, Alastair nodded, fighting the joy that surged through his heart, afraid to trust it. Then his gaze fell to the small item in the man's hand, and his blood froze. "What is that?" he demanded, his hand rising to point at the small straw flower the Englishman was shifting from hand to hand.

Pausing, Beth's brother looked down. "Tillie made it for me." Again, he turned it in his hand.

In shock, Alastair stared at the small, blue flower as his world came crashing down around him. Was this it? Was today the day?

His gaze rose to meet the Englishman's narrowed eyes. "Did my wife see it?"

The man nodded, glancing down at the small item in his hand before meeting Alastair's gaze once more. "She did. In fact, she reacted much like you. Shocked somehow." He shook his head. "But she wouldn't say why. Is there anything I can do? What is going on?"

As the breath lodged in his throat, Alastair found himself stumbling backwards, barely aware that the Englishman was still speaking to him. He turned and rushed back down the corridor, not knowing where to go. Where was Deidre? Had she left for the ruins?

Everything around him retreated into the background as his feet carried him onward, his heart hammering in his chest. What was he to do?

When he all but stumbled by their chamber, he found the door ajar. Pushing it open, Alastair rushed inside, only to find the room empty. Still, as his gaze swept over the bed they had shared the night before, he found a piece of parchment lying there. Moving forward, he picked it up, knowing even before his gaze settled on the page that it was the letter Moira had sent Deidre over two years ago.

The letter about the blue flower.

Closing his eyes, Alastair sank down onto the bed, his hands crumpling up the page as his heart broke with the sudden loss.

She was gone!

His wife had left!

Deidre!

All strength left his body as his heart cried out in pain. Even though he had fought to keep his distance, her loss destroyed him. Especially after the previous night, when he had finally allowed himself a shred of hope. He had been a fool!

A part of him wanted to chase after her, and yet, he knew that it would be selfish. If Moira had seen her happy, then he would have to trust in that. Always had his sister's visions come true; not always the way they had seemed at first, but in a sense. If Deidre found love and happiness, he needed to step back.

He needed to let her go.

Even if it killed him.

"Here, ye are," came Connor's booming voice from the doorway. "I've been looking all over for ye."

His cousin's breath came fast, and Alastair looked up, the hairs on the back of his neck rising in trepidation. Something was wrong! "Why?"

Connor stepped into the room. "A messenger from Clan

MacDrummond arrived with a letter for ye." He held up the item in question, his dark gaze meaningful as it met Alastair's. "'Tis from Moira. The man said she had told him to put it in yer hands without delay."

Alastair swallowed as his skin began to crawl, with what he could not say.

Long ago, he and Moira had been close before her betrayal had ripped them apart. Unable to forgive her, to place his trust in her again, Alastair had pushed her away, hoping that the pain would lessen if he pretended it was not there. It had been years since they had last spoken, since they had last seen one another, and yet, his heart still ached for the sister he had lost.

She had always known what to say. Her counsel a guiding hand whenever he knew not what to do. How was it that she knew to reach out to him in his darkest hour? Had she had another vision?

Pushing to his feet, Alastair all but ripped the envelope out of his cousin's hand. His own trembled as he freed the parchment within, his gaze drawn to her delicate handwriting.

Dearest Brother,

A part of me fears that you will burn this letter without opening it while another still has hope that not all is lost. If you're reading these lines now, then there must still be some small part of you that believes.

Whatever doubts you may have, please believe that I never meant to hurt you. I love you as I always have, and I want nothing more but to see you happy again.

Please, heed my words! Not for my sake, but for your own.

Last night, my dreams took me to a moment which has not yet come to pass. A moment that made me question the meaning of the blue flower. At first, I thought it a bad omen for you and Deidre. I felt sadness and sorrow. I saw a new love for her, and so I feared that something would rip the two of you apart.

However, in last night's dream, I felt your heart overflow with joy and love. I saw you happy, truly happy, and I know without a doubt that there is no happiness found in this life for you without Deidre by your side.

I still cannot say what the blue flower means, what love it will guide her to, but I now believe it does not mean that you'll lose her. Perhaps it speaks of an old love rediscovered. Perhaps it is something else.

But I know in my heart that you must not give up. Don't let her go, Alastair! I beg you for I'm certain you'll regret it for the rest of your life.

Your loving sister,

Moira

Tears stood in Alastair's eyes as he stared at the blurring lines written in his sister's delicate hand, and in that moment, he no longer doubted her, he no longer felt any anger or betrayal toward her, he no longer wanted her gone.

He wanted her back.

"Are ye all right?" came Connor's voice, now soft and quiet, almost fearful as his hand settled on Alastair's shoulder. "Ye look the fright."

"I need to go." All exhaustion fell from him, and his body hummed with the need to move. Without another word, Alastair rushed out the door, folding up his sister's letter before he settled it in his pocket, next to his daughter's auburn curl. He would reach out to her, he promised himself as well as her, but first, he needed to go after his wife.

No matter where Fate would guide them, he refused to believe it would guide them down separate paths. They belonged together. They always had, and they always would.

What a fool he had been to ever doubt that!

Chapter Eight

A HUSBAND'S CLAIM

No one had seen her white mare-Aurora had all but vanished from her box-and so Deidre had reluctantly saddled the grey gelding, determined to seek out the ruins and finally find an answer to the questions swirling in her mind. She could not deny her curiosity, but she had also grown weary of this mysterious prediction. She knew that it pained Alastair, and she needed to put his mind at ease. Only then would he be able to forget and begin again.

Only then would they have a chance.

Deidre needed answers, and she would find them.

Pushing the grey gelding across the snow-covered meadow, she looked toward the horizon. The sky glistened in a clear blue, welcoming the bright sun as it shone down upon the frozen world. Its soft golden rays lingered on the crumbled ruins in the distance like a guide shining a light to where she needed to go. Her skin prickled from the cold, and her breath came fast as she drew closer to the moment that would determine her future.

A neigh behind her drew her attention, and Deidre turned to look over her shoulder.

A rider was fast approaching, his blond hair whipping in the wind as he leaned over his horse's neck. Alastair! What on earth was he doing here?

Pulling on her reins, Deidre slowed her gelding, bracing herself for her husband's anger. Did he think she was leaving him? Nothing could be further from the truth!

Still, the thought that he had come after her warmed her heart, and she could not prevent a little smile from showing on her face. He loved her! No matter what he said he loved her!

Pulling his gelding to a rather abrupt halt, Alastair jumped from his mount's back. His face looked strained, his blue eyes fixed on hers as he strode toward her. Determination lingered in every step, and she saw his jaw tense with a fierceness she had rarely seen. What was he about?

"What are ye doing out here?" Deidre asked, a chill travelling up and down her spine as he advanced, his steps not slowing. "Why are ye-?"

Her question was cut short when Alastair reached for her, his strong hands clasping her arms and pulling her out of the saddle. She all but fell against his broad chest, his arms crushing her in a tight embrace that had her feet dangling in the air.

When he finally set her down, his blue eyes all but burnt into hers, not the slightest flicker of doubt in them. "I willna let ye go, do ye hear? Ye're mine, Deidre. Mine!" Then his head swooped down and his mouth came down on hers, staking his claim in the most primal manner.

Deidre gasped at the urgency in him. One arm clamped around her waist, holding her to him, while the other slid along her jaw and then down to her neck. His skin was chilled as it brushed against hers, and she felt another shiver dance down her limbs. Then his hand slipped inside her hood until it settled on the back of her head, angling her so he could deepen their kiss.

All thought fled Deidre's mind as she clung to her husband, and heartbeat by heartbeat, the world began to right itself. Alastair had always been a man of few words, but the ones he did say held deep meaning. More so, she understood the way his hands held on to her, unyielding and yet gentle. She understood the desperate longing in his kiss and felt her heart ache with the same need. Her hands curled into his coat, and she pushed herself up onto her toes, striving to be closer.

A low rumble in his throat told her that her response pleased him, that she had given him the answer he had needed, the answer he had come out here to claim. His kiss grew gentler, slower before a sigh left his lips, and he rested his forehead against hers, eyes closed, his warm breath brushing over her chilled skin.

"I love ye, too," Deidre whispered, a deep smile tugging on the corners of her mouth as she looked up at her husband.

His eyes opened, their blue shining with deep intensity as he stared down at her. His hands still held her as tightly as before, not allowing her to move, to step away from him. "Ye left," he whispered, and she felt his thumb brush over the edge of her jaw.

"I left the castle," Deidre told him, needing him to understand that nothing in this world could ever make her leave his side. "Not ye. Never."

Alastair glanced over her shoulder at the ruins in the distance. Then his gaze settled back on hers, a question burning there that needed an answer.

Deidre swallowed. "I need to know." His hands tensed, and she gasped at the sudden pressure against her ribs. "I need to know what Moira's vision means, and ye do as well." Her gaze held his patiently as she waited for her words to be absorbed. "We canna go on not knowing. There'll always be doubt, not in my heart, but in yers. I can see it in yer eyes."

His breath came fast as he stared at her, and yet, little by little the grip he held her in lessened.

Cupping a hand to his cheek, Deidre smiled at him. "I am yers as ye are mine. That'll never change. Have faith. In me. In us." She rose up to plant a gentle kiss on his lips. "There can never be another. Never."

A deep breath of utter relief rushed from his body as he buried his face in the crook of her neck, his arms holding her gently, safe and warm. "I love ye, Deidre," he whispered, his lips brushing her neck, sending a tingle of anticipation through her.

Later, she cautioned herself. There would be time for that later. Now, they needed answers.

"Will ye come with me?" she asked, brushing a hand up the side of his neck. "Will ye come and see for yerself what has been haunting ye?"

Again, his eyes met hers. "Ye're mine," he said once more as though to reassure himself.

Deidre smiled. "Aye. Always."

Chapter Nine

THE OLD RUINS

Unable to tear his gaze from his wife, Alastair pushed his mount on, the ruins looming higher with each step they took. His heart ached with the need to hold her, to take her away from this place, this threat, and yet, a part of him understood the wisdom of her choice. They needed to know. *He* needed to know.

Sliding out of the saddle, they slipped their horses' reins over a shoulder-high boulder, standing like a sentinel at the outer wall of the crumbling keep. Then Alastair drew his wife's hand through the crook of his arm, needing to feel her, to have her close.

Deidre smiled up at him, her small hand brushing over the side of his face. "Dunna be afraid," she whispered, snuggling closer. "All shall be well."

Alastair could only hope so, wishing with all his heart that Moira was right, that what she had seen would come to pass, that they would find happiness.

Together.

Was there any other kind?

Not to his knowledge.

As they stepped farther into the old ruins, a soft nicker drifted to their ears and a moment later Deidre's mare trotted into their path, her white coat almost hiding her in the bright snow-covered landscape.

"Aurora!" Deidre exclaimed, rushing toward the gentle mare. "What are ye doing here? I've been worried."

Alastair frowned, only now remembering that he had found Aurora missing before Deidre had even left the castle. He glanced over his shoulder at the two horses they had left behind a few steps back, his eyes settling on the grey gelding.

In the moment he had come upon his wife, his thoughts had been focused elsewhere to realise that she had not been on Aurora. He looked back at the white mare, noting the way the saddle hung on her back as though not fastened properly.

Alastair strode closer as the little hairs on the back of his neck began to rise. Something was wrong!

"There's blood here," Deidre exclaimed, her eyes wide as she stared at the mare's saddle. Then her gaze moved to him. "What is going on?"

Alastair shook his head, his gaze moving over their surroundings as he drew the sword at his side. "We're not alone," he whispered, his steps carrying him back to his wife. He grasped her arm and pulled her behind him as his gaze continued to search the snow-covered ruins. "There are footprints here."

Exhaling slowly, Alastair willed his thundering heart to calm as he continued to sweep his gaze over their surroundings. His skin crawled with the threat that might be lying in wait somewhere nearby, and he cursed himself for giving in, for not stopping them from seeking out this place. "We should leave," he muttered under his breath, afraid to see harm come to his wife. He had only just gotten her back. He would not lose her now. Who knew who was lingering in these ruins?

Beside him, Deidre shook her head. "We canna. Something is wrong."

"Aye, 'tis why we should leave."

Again, Deidre shook her head before she suddenly stilled, her eyes going wide.

"What?" Alastair hissed.

Her eyes met his, still wide and filled with... "I canna say, but..." Her gaze turned toward the small shelter where Alastair had come upon her the day of their guests' arrival. It stood off to the side, its remaining walls hiding the inside from their view. Whoever had taken Aurora to come here, was this where they were waiting?

"Who do ye think it is?" Alastair whispered, knowing that it had to be someone from the castle.

Deidre shrugged. "I dunna know, but whoever it is needs help."

Alastair frowned.

His wife's warm eyes met his before she glanced at the blood-stained saddle atop Aurora.

Swallowing, Alastair nodded. "Aye, but stay behind me."

Slowly, they moved forward, step by step following the prints left behind in the snow. As they drew closer to the small shelter, they found more blood droplets, shining brightly like little beacons on the snow-covered ground. Alastair felt his muscles tense, his breath lodging in his throat. He wished he could put his wife on a horse and send her back home, but he knew she would never leave. Her big heart would not allow her. He could only hope that the threat he feared was not one after all. That his wife was right, and they would come upon someone in need of their help.

Approaching the half-crumbled wall, Alastair drew in a deep breath, his muscles readying themselves for whatever might lay ahead. He gripped his sword tighter, then surged around the corner, exposing only himself.

The moment his gaze fell on the inside of the small shelter, he almost dropped his sword. His blood ran cold, and a piercing pain surged through his heart.

"Oh, no!" Deidre gasped behind him before she lunged forward, then dropped onto her knees, her hands reaching for the small babe.

Half-leaning against the back wall, Alastair saw a young woman. A woman he had seen before, and although it took him a few moments to place her face, he finally remembered where he had seen her. She had arrived with their guests a few days prior. Miss Harmon, was it? Tillie's and Jonathan's governess?

Her eyes were closed, and her skin looked awfully pale. Still, he could see the faint pulse beating in her neck. A pulse that seemed to be slowing as her chest rose and fell with each laboured breath. A slight shiver shook her, and her lips looked blue, from the cold or the loss of blood Alastair could not say. Her skirts were stained dark red, her blood seeping onto the ground in a wide circle around her. It was evident that she had just given birth, and it was equally clear that she was now standing at Death's door.

As Deidre had a few years back.

Agony gripped Alastair as old memories came rushing back. Deidre, pale and almost lifeless, on the bed, his stillborn son in his arms. He had been born prematurely, and Alastair still remembered how small he had been, almost fitting into the palm of his hand.

"He's alive," Deidre exclaimed, her words shaking Alastair from the stupor that had gripped him. She looked over her shoulder, her eyes meeting his for the barest of moments, before she once more turned to the infant.

Swallowing, Alastair crouched down beside her, his gaze travelling over the boy's small body, his skin stained red with blood. Still, there was a paleness about him that spoke of a fight soon to be lost.

"He's cold," Deidre muttered before her hands reached for her coat, unbuttoning it. She pulled it off, then turned her back to him. "Open my laces. Quick!"

Stumped, Alastair did as he was bid, his fingers working with an efficiency that surprised him. A moment later, she pulled her dress half off her shoulders, her skin puckering as the cold wind brushed over it. "What are ye-?"

With a mother's practised hand, Deidre scooped up the small babe and settled him against her chest, carefully sliding his shivering body under her dress. Then she urged Alastair to fasten her laces once more, holding the child in place, before she slipped on her coat, wrapping it around them both. Her arms wrapped around him, rubbing his back through the fabric, warming him as best as she could. Then her gaze moved to his mother. "Is she alive?"

Alastair nodded, then rose and moved closer, checking the woman's pulse. "But not for much longer," he warned as his gaze met Deidre's.

Her jaw tightened and she blinked away tears. "We need to take her back to the castle. She needs Morag."

At the mention of the old healer who lived hidden somewhere in the woods, Alastair nodded. No one quite knew how to find her, but she had a knack for appearing whenever she was needed. Alastair had no doubt that if they managed to get Miss Harmon back to the castle, Morag would find them there.

Shrugging off his coat, he wrapped it around the half-conscious woman. A low moan escaped her lips as he moved her, bundling her up as best as he could. Then he leaned her back against the wall. "I'll get the horses."

Alastair barely felt the cold as he strode back out into the freezing wind, quickly leading over the two horses they had left by the outer wall of the ruins. When he returned, he found Deidre crouched by Miss Harmon's side, her right hand brushing over the woman's arm while the other held on to the child. "Ye need to be strong now. Yer son needs ye. I promise I'll keep him warm for ye, but ye need to hold on." Tears rolled down her cheeks, and Alastair wished he could spare his wife the reminder of her own losses.

There had been too many.

Far too many.

How many more could his delicate wife bear? He could only hope that this would not break her.

Chapter Ten

A MOTHER'S STRENGTH

S ettled on the grey gelding, Deidre held on tightly to the child resting against her chest. His body had warmed, and now he slowly began to stir. His arms and legs moved, sometimes slowly and sometimes in soft jerks. Deidre could feel his chest rise and fall with each breath and his little mouth moving against her skin, searching.

He needed to nurse.

Glancing across at Sophie-or Miss Harmon as Alastair insisted on calling her-bundled up in her husband's arms, Deidre knew that the woman was far too weak to nurse her son. Once they returned to the castle, she would have to find some milk to feed him before he grew too weak.

Deidre's arms tightened around the boy, and she swallowed the lump in her throat, willing herself not to picture his small, lifeless body. "I'll take care of ye," she whispered to the top of his head, hidden deep in the folds of her coat. "Ye needna worry. All will be well."

Aurora, her saddle still askew, trotted behind them as they slowly made their way back toward Greystone Castle. The journey was long and arduous, a lingering fear that they would not make it in time always present.

Deidre often met her husband's gaze and saw there the same fear, the same urgency she felt in her own heart. If only they could rush their horses!

However, Sophie lay slack in Alastair's arms, one of Deidre's petticoats wedged between her legs in the hopes of stemming the flow of blood. Still, whenever Deidre looked behind them, she spotted droplets of blood dripping onto the clear, white snow as though leaving a trail for someone to follow.

"She's growing weaker," Alastair mumbled, agony in his gaze as it met hers. She could hear the warning in his voice, urging her not to get her hopes up. He feared for her. Deidre knew that, but she would not give up. She could not. Not until all was truly lost.

"I'll ride ahead and send for help," she told him, knowing if she held the boy close to her body, she could push her gelding to move faster without endangering the child.

Alastair's jaw tightened, his gaze fixed on hers, and she could see that he wanted to object. That he worried about her. But he did not say a word. He merely nodded, his gaze warm and comforting, urging her to be careful.

Deidre cast him a grateful smile, then she wrapped her right hand tightly around the child before urging her gelding into a slow trot. Moving with the horse, Deidre managed to keep the boy from being jostled too much, her eyes fixed on the tall walls in the distance. "We can make it, *leannan*. Hold on to me. I'll see ye safe."

Soft murmurs tumbled from her lips as she pushed onward, her gaze fixed on her target, watching it grow larger with each step her gelding took. Soon, she could see people moving about the village. She waved her other arm, calling out to draw their attention.

Some stopped in their paths, and then after an agonisingly long moment, one spun around and darted up the path to the castle. Moments later, men appeared on the parapet wall before distant shouts drifted to her ears.

Deidre pushed onward, her heart growing lighter now that she was so close. Her gaze remained fixed on the castle, and a breath of relief rushed from her lungs when she saw a rider suddenly charge out of the gate, heading straight toward her. Even from the distance, Deidre recognised the tall, bear-like stature of her cousin Connor.

His horse's hooves thundered closer, eating up the ground, before he pulled the black beast to a halt right in front of her. "What's happened, Lass?" he demanded, his gaze wide and fearful as it swept over her. "Ye look the fright. Where's Alastair?" His eyes drifted to the horizon, but there was nothing yet for them to see.

"We need a cart," she rushed to say just as the babe in her arms began to squirm in earnest, soft wails echoing from his lips. "Now! Go!"

Connor frowned at the sound of the babe, but then nodded, urging his mount back up the path. Deidre noted that he had not bothered to put a saddle on the beast, but merely thrown on a bridle.

Before she had even reached the gate, a small cart rumbled out, accompanied by a group of clansmen as well as her cousin. "Where to, Lass?"

"Toward the ruins," Deidre rushed to say before Connor waved the men onward. "'Tis Sophie. Miss Harmon," she told him then. "She's had a babe. We found her at the ruins, bleeding, barely conscious. She needs Morag. We need to send for her."

Running a hand over his face, Connor shook his head, a disbelieving smile tickling the corners of his mouth. "The old crow is already here," he chuckled. "Said the wind had whispered to her that she'd be needed here."

For a moment, Deidre was stunned before she remembered that the old woman had always come when she had been needed. Long since had Deidre suspected that Morag possessed a similar gift to Moira's. Who knew? For *the old crow* had always wrapped herself in silence, a mysterious twinkle in her seeing eyes.

"I need to see to the babe," Deidre told Connor before she urged her gelding through the gate. The moment she pulled to a halt in the courtyard, her cousin was there beside her, his huge hands lifting her and the child out of the saddle and setting her gently onto the ground.

The boy was now screaming at the top of his lungs, and Deidre all but ran up the stairs to the great hall. Her family met her there, their eyes widening at the sound of the child's cries. Rhona, Connor's mother and the heart of the Brunwood family, quickly distributed tasks as she pulled Deidre down the corridor and toward her chamber.

"He needs milk," Deidre told her aunt as she unbuttoned her coat.

Rhona pushed open the door and led Deidre inside. "And he shall have some," she stated in a voice that brooked no argument. If ever there had been a woman who could move the earth, it was Rhona. She was a quiet woman, often kept to the background, but when crisis struck, she stood tall, her calm presence seeing to all those under her care. "Dunna worry, dear. He shall be fine."

"I hope so," Deidre whispered as she carefully lifted the boy from her chest and gently placed him in Rhona's waiting arms, a warm blanket wrapping about him. Her skin and dress where stained with dried blood as was the babe's. Still, the way he waved his arms made her heart soar.

A moment later, women rushed in bringing warmed milk as well as clean linens and hot water with a small tub. Rhona handed the boy to Deidre and all but pushed her into the armchair by the hearth. Then she handed her the milk. "Go ahead and feed him, dear. I'll see to the rest."

For a few moments, the chamber exploded in a flurry of movements as all was set up. Then Rhona chased the other women out before turning to Deidre. "I'll go see to his mother," she said, a gentle smile on her face. "Call me if ye need anything."

The moment the door closed behind her aunt, Deidre felt the whole world fall away. Her eyes were glued to the boy's little face as he drank hungrily, his right fist clenched in her sleeve. He had big, blue eyes and...a tuft of red hair on the top of his head.

Deidre's heart clenched at the memory of her own child. Little Rory with her auburn curls!

Her hand brushed gently over the boy's soft face, his skin still covered in dried blood. Then she touched the pad of her finger to a red lock, lying curled upon his head. It felt soft and warm and wonderful.

Tears began streaming down her face as she rocked him. "All is well, *leannan*. Yer mother will soon hold ye in her arms. Dunna worry. All shall be well."

Chapter Eleven

AN ECHO OF THE PAST

The moment Morag shoved him with her bony hands out of the chamber and told him he was no longer needed, Alastair breathed a sigh of relief for he could no longer bear to look at Miss Harmon. The sight of her made his heart twist in agony, and he could barely keep at bay the memories that lingered nearby. He prayed she would live, but he could not hold her hand during this fight.

Exhausted, he stumbled down the corridor toward their chamber, only to pull up short as Deidre's soft voice drifted to his ears. She was humming a lullaby she had often sung to their daughter and his heart clenched with longing.

Without doubt, he knew what he would find on the other side of the door. He knew he would find his wife with a child in her arms, a soft smile on her lips and joy in her eyes. Only this child was not hers.

Alastair sighed, knowing that more heartache lay in their future. Then he pushed open the door and stepped over the threshold.

Deidre's warm gaze found his, and the smile that lit up her face nearly brought him to his knees. "He's well," she whispered, rocking the sleeping boy in her arms. "He drank the whole bottle." She brushed a loving finger over his little forehead. "Aye, ye were a hungry little lad."

Alastair swallowed as his gaze drifted over the sleeping child. A part of him uttered a warning, urging him to be cautious, but he could not keep his eyes away. Slowly, he stepped closer, noting the boy's warm skin, glowing rosy in the soft light of the room, now clean after a good washing. His eyes were slightly slanted. His thin lashes resting against his cheek bones as he slept peacefully, his little fist curled around one of Deidre's fingers.

"Look at his hair," Deidre urged him, a smile on her lips and her eyes brimming with tears. "'Tis red, like Rory's."

Alastair swallowed as he knelt beside them. "Aye, he's beautiful."

Deidre sighed, the breath shuddering past her lips. Still, the soft smile stayed on her lips, bravely fighting against the sorrow that lingered. "Will ye hold him?" she asked then. "So, I can change and wash."

Alastair's heart clenched in panic, and yet, he could not deny that a part of him *wanted* to hold the child.

Pushing to his feet, he gently took the babe from her arms. The boy stirred slightly, a soft sigh leaving his lips, before he settled contentedly into the crook of Alastair's arm. He was warm and soft and so very much alive.

He felt like Rory.

Seating himself in the armchair, Alastair alternately watched his wife and the child in his arms, a part of him crying out at the sense of family that washed over him while another urged him to reach out and hold on to it, not allowing it to slip away.

That night, he slept with his wife in his arms and the child tucked safely between them. They had tried to settle him in Rory's old crib, but he would start crying every time they set him down and only calm the moment they settled him back in their arms.

"He feels lonely," Deidre whispered. "He misses his mother."

Alastair understood his wife's need to remind herself of the reality of their situation for a part of him wished they could remain in this dream as well.

Over the next few days, they settled into a delicate routine caring for the child. Morag had seen to the boy's mother, remaining at her side as Miss Harmon was still very weak. Fortunately, the old healer had managed to stem the blood flow and was now cautiously opti-mistic that the woman would recover.

"Can we see her?" Deidre asked on the third day, the boy in her arms. "I'm certain she'll want to meet her son."

Alastair had cautioned her, raising the question of why Miss Harmon had set out on her own, placing herself as well as her child in danger. Deidre, however, had waved his objections aside, unable to contemplate the notion that a mother-any mother-would not wish to see her child.

"Aye, she's awake," Morag replied, watchful eyes drifting to the boy. Still, Alastair thought to see a hint of apprehension in them. "Perhaps the sight of him will rouse her spirits."

Smiling, Deidre stepped up to the door, then waited for Alastair to open it. Slowly, she moved inside, gesturing at him to follow. "Sophie," she whispered, her eyes gliding over the woman in the bed. Her skin was still pale, but no longer ashen. Her lips once more held a little colour, and her chest rose and fell with even breaths. "Sophie, I've brought ye yer son."

Remaining by the foot of the bed, Alastair watched as Deidre strode closer, then sat down at the edge of the mattress. "He's well as I promised ye."

Miss Harmon's eyes fluttered open, and for a moment, she seemed thoroughly disoriented. Then her gaze drifted over Deidre before dropping lower, touching upon the auburn-haired head of her child. Instantly, she tensed, her fingers clenching into the bedclothes. "No," the word left her lips on a shuddering breath, panic widening her eyes. "No, take him away. I don't wish to see him."

Alastair tensed, and he saw his wife still as well. The smile slid from her face, replaced by a look of utter confusion, her arms tightening on the child as though to shield him from the harsh truth. "But ye dunna understand," Deidre began gently, lifting the child so Miss Harmon could see his lovely face. "He is well. Ye dunna need to fear for him. He is well."

Still, the look of terror on the woman's face did not change. She all but tried to push herself to the other side of the bed, her arms trembling with the effort. Her breath came fast now, and Alastair feared she might lose consciousness if this continued much longer.

"Deidre," he said softly before rounding the bed and coming to stand by her shoulder.

Her eyes held sorrow as she looked up from the boy's face, a hint of agitation coming to it as he began to squirm, no doubt upset by the harsh voice filled with panic that drifted to his ears.

"Hand him to me," Alastair said, kneeling beside his wife. "I promise to keep him safe." His gaze drifted to Miss Harmon's wide eyes. "Ye'll speak to her."

Nodding, Deidre handed him the child, the pad of her thumb brushing over the boy's brow before her hands fell away and she turned toward Miss Harmon.

With the boy's soft weight settled in his arms, Alastair took one last look at the child's mother before leaving the room. In his heart, he could not understand how any parent could refuse their child. Still, a part of him knew that sometimes there was a good reason why a woman could not bond with her babe.

Poor Miss Harmon.

Chapter Twelve

DARK MEMORIES

As shocked as she was to hear Sophie reject her son, Deidre was not blind to the signs of terror, of sorrow in the woman's fearful face. Her eyes were wide, and yet, brimming with tears while her hands could not seem to relinquish their tense hold on the bedclothes as though they were a lifeline keeping her afloat.

"What happened?" Deidre asked softly as she carefully reached out and placed her hand on Sophie's.

The young woman's eyes closed, and tears rolled down her cheeks. "I never wanted this. I did not know what to do." Her lips began to quiver, and the hand under Deidre's tensed further.

"I know," Deidre murmured softly, scooting closer and gently rubbing her hand up and down the woman's arm. "I know."

For a long while, they sat in silence as Sophie fought down the panic that held her in its clutches. Little by little, her body began to relax and her breathing evened. Still, when she finally opened her eyes, the sorrow Deidre had seen there still shone with the same painful acuteness as before.

"Will ye tell me what happened, Sophie?" Deidre asked again, knowing only too well that pain had a way of settling in one's bones if it was kept a secret. It was far better to share it and thus rob it of at least some of its power. "Did ye know ye were with child when ye came here?"

Swallowing, Sophie nodded. "I didn't want to go, but I couldn't..." Shaking her head, she closed her eyes. "Lady Whitworth has always been so good to me. I couldn't bear the thought of her thinking that..." Again, her voice trailed off.

"Thinking what?" Deidre pressed, squeezing the woman's hand. "Who's the child's father?"

Sophie flinched as though slapped, her eyes going wide with memories dark and painful.

Understanding found Deidre, and her teeth gritted together at the sight of the other woman's pain. "Is he still in yer life? Do ye still need to fear him?"

Sophie drew in a shuddering breath. "No. It was a house party, a former acquaintance of Lord Radcliff's." She swallowed. "I haven't seen him since." She sighed, and her hand clasped Deidre's. "I tried to forget, but then..."

Deidre nodded, thinking of John and the man he had once been. The rake. *He* had changed, but it would seem his old acquaintance had seen no need to. "Ye realised ye were with child."

Fresh tears tumbled down the woman's cheeks as sobs tore from her throat. "I did not know what to do, and then we came here, and when the pain started, all I could think about was that I needed to get away." Her eyes were wide as her hand clutched Deidre's harder. "I sneaked outside and got a horse. I thought if I could get to a nearby village..." She shook her head. "I didn't want anyone to know. I wasn't thinking. I was...I..."

"Ye were afraid," Deidre finished for her. "Of course, ye were. There's no shame in that, Sophie. No one here would blame ye for anything." She glanced over her shoulder at the door. "Lady Whitworth, Adelaide, is a kind and understanding woman. She wouldna have blamed ye or looked down at ye. Believe me. These people out there," she squeezed Sophie's hand, casting her a warm smile, "they take care of one another. They're family, to me as well as to ye."

Dropping her gaze, Sophie shook her head. "I'm only the governess. They wouldn't-"

"Ye've taken care of Tillie since she was a babe?"

Glancing up, Sophie nodded.

"Then ye're family," Deidre told her, her gaze drifting to the straw figurines on the woman's nightstand. "Tillie made these for ye?"

Sophie nodded, a soft smile coming to her face. "She's such a sweet child, always taking care of others." She sighed. "She made these for me to help me feel better. Of course, she could not have known that..."

Deidre patted her hand. "I understand that ye were afraid, but ye need to know that ye're not alone. Has Adelaide come to speak to ye?"

Sophie nodded once more. "She has, but I pretended to be asleep." She pressed her lips together. "I could not face her."

"If ye want, I will speak to her," Deidre offered. "Explain everything. Ye will see that she will stand by ye. She will make sure that that man will never get anywhere near ye again."

Although doubt still clung to Sophie's face, her muscles began to relax, and a spark of hope came to her wide eyes. "You truly think so."

"I know so," Deidre told the other woman, knowing that there was nothing more powerful to battle fear than someone who would stand by one's side. "She will help ye as ye've helped her with her children. Now, she'll help ye with yers."

Panic widened Sophie's eyes once more. "No, I do not wish to see him. I can't!"

Deidre sighed. "Why not? He's but a babe. A sweet, innocent, little lad with a beautiful tuft of red hair."

A shudder of revulsion shook Sophie, her jaw clenching as she fought against the panic that welled up in her heart. "Like him," she gritted out. "Red hair like...like him." Her eyes closed. Then she pinched them together as though trying to rid herself of the memories. "I can't look at him. I simply can't." Her eyes opened then, once again brimming with tears. "I know that he is innocent. I know that he deserves to be loved, but..." She shook her head, deep sorrow in her gaze. "I cannot be his mother. If I tried, I would only fail him. He would know that..."

Deidre felt her own heart clench at the heartbreak in Sophie's gaze.

"Do ye not at least wish to try? The day might come that ye will regret ye gave him up. At least hold him and-"

"No!" Sophie replied with a surprisingly strong voice. "I'd rather risk regrets of my own than to force them on him. This is the one thing I can do for him." She inhaled a deep breath as her hands reached for Deidre's, her eyes intent and full of purpose. "I need to let him go. It's the only way I can give him a chance at happiness."

The thought of giving up one's child-no matter the circumstances-was something Deidre could not grasp. A hollowness spread through her chest at the thought, and in her mind, she saw the little boy's soft face, eyes closed in slumber as he had lain in her arms.

So precious.

"Do you want him?"

Blinking, Deidre stared at the young woman, her heart beginning to hammer in her chest as Sophie's words slowly sank in. "What?"

The young woman swallowed. "I've heard of...your loss," she whispered. "I know he cannot replace your daughter, but if you think you could love him..."

Deidre surged to her feet as fear gripped her heart, squeezing it until it hurt. Her feet carried her away from the bed, to the window, then the other side of the room and back, her breath coming in panting gasps that she feared she might faint. Her hands rose to rub over her face, and she found her cheeks wet with tears.

"If you don't think you can..." Sophie sighed, leaning back against the pillow, exhaustion washing over her face. "I understand. I only thought...perhaps it was Fate that you were the ones to find us up there."

Shock froze Deidre's limbs as she stared at the young woman, her mind drawn back to a day long ago. A day a letter had arrived. A letter telling her that on the day marked by a blue flower, she would find a great love up by the old ruins!

The breath lodged in Deidre's throat, and her jaw began to quiver. "'Tis him," she gasped, hands clasped over her mouth, fear and hope mingling in her heart as Moira's words echoed in her mind. "'Twas him I was meant to find."

A slight frown came to Sophie's face as she watched her. "Does that mean you want him?"

Trembling, Deidre nodded. "Aye, I do."

"Then he's yours."

Chapter Thirteen

A DAUGHTER'S GIFT

Seated in the armchair by the hearth in their chamber, Alastair rocked the little boy in his arms. His eyes shone in a bright blue, wonder and awe resting in them as he stared up at Alastair's face, his little hands opening and closing.

Gently, Alastair ran a finger over the boy's palm, and instantly his hand clamped shut, trapping Alastair's finger with his own. "Well done, little lad," he chuckled, remembering how he had often played this game with his daughter.

Tears came to his eyes and he let them fall. "Her name was Rory," he told the little boy, his wide blue eyes fixed on Alastair's face as though he was listening intently. "She was a bonny, little lass with hair as red as yers." His gaze trailed over the child's auburn curls. "Ye would've liked her. She always slept like a rock, but she could also scream like a banshee." Another chuckle rose in his throat, and Alastair wondered why it was that he could suddenly remember his daughter with fondness and not only with sorrow.

The boy cooed softly, the corners of his mouth twitching.

"Are ye tired, little lad?"

As though in answer, a wide yawn stretched over the little boy's face and his eyes fluttered closed.

Settling him deeper into the crook of his arm, Alastair rose to his feet, gently rocking the child as he hummed Deidre's lullaby under his breath. Warmth filled his heart, and Alastair remembered well the many peaceful moments he had spent with his wife and child. If only life had taken a different turn.

If only.

Looking down at the sleeping little boy, Alastair could not help but wish that he would never have to let him go. He was not Rory. He was his own person, a little child, who called to Alastair, tugging on his heart and reawakening old longings.

"Is he asleep?"

Turning around, Alastair found his wife quietly closing the door. He had not even heard her approach, so lost had he been in his musings. "Aye, he just now drifted off." His gaze rose and he met her eyes, red-rimmed and still brimming with unshed tears. "Are ye all right? What did Miss Harmon say? Does she want to see him?"

Deidre's jaw trembled as she inhaled a shuddering breath, her gaze flitting about the chamber before it settled on his. Alastair could not deny the gooseflesh that prickled his skin at the look in his wife's eyes. Something had happened. Something deeply unsettling...and yet there was the hint of a smile teasing her lips.

As Deidre walked over to them, her gaze dropped to the little boy in his arms, and she brushed a gentle hand over his auburn curls. Then she sighed, and her gaze hardened, grew sorrowful, before she looked up at him. "She canna bear to look at him," his wife whispered, "because the man who fathered him forced himself on her."

Alastair's teeth gritted together in outrage as he willed himself to remain still so as not to disturb the lad's slumber.

Deidre nodded, her other hand coming to rest on his arm. "He had red hair."

A long breath rushed from Alastair's lungs, and his gaze was drawn to the innocent, little boy sleeping peacefully in his arms. "What now?" he whispered, the thought of a child all alone was a painful reminder that the world was not a perfect place.

Reaching up, Deidre brushed a tear from his cheek, a soft smile on her face. "I spoke to Adelaide and explained what had happened. She was shocked. Matthew was furious. They promised to look after her and speak to John about...that man. Apparently, he was an old acquaintance of his."

Alastair nodded, anger clenching his jaw. "I can only hope he'll thrash him within an inch of his life. He'd deserve far worse." A low growl rumbled in his throat at the thought of the strong preying on the weak. That was not the world he wanted to live in, the world he had wanted his daughter to live in. "What about the lad? Will Adelaide and Matthew take him in?"

Looking up, Alastair found the breath lodge in his throat at the wide smile that rested on his wife's lovely face. Her eyes shone with utter joy as she moved closer, her hands settling gently upon his arms, brushing down his sleeves until one settled on the boy's head. "Do ye want him?"

Alastair felt as though someone had punched him in the gut, and for a moment, he feared he would drop the child. He only barely managed to stay on his feet, his eyes wide and staring.

Deidre swallowed. "She canna be his mother. She knows she canna love him the way he deserves, but she wants him to be happy." Tears rolled down her cheeks. "And loved." Her hand squeezed his arm as her eyes burnt into his. "Do ye think ye could love him? He's not Rory, and I dunna want him to be. He'll be her little brother, and we'll tell him all about his big sister." A sob tore from her lips. "She'll not be forgotten. Never."

"Take him," was all Alastair managed to say before his muscles went slack.

Deidre's sure hands swooped in to take the boy, who made a little fussing noise in his sleep at being jostled from one to the other. Then, however, he sighed deeply, one little hand curling into Deidre's dress as she rocked him gently, the old lullaby once more on her lips.

Alastair stumbled back to the armchair he had only vacated moments earlier and sank into it, his legs no longer able to keep him upright. Overwhelmed, he listened to the blood rushing in his ears and felt his heart pounding in his chest as though wishing to break free.

"I know," Deidre whispered beside him, her hand coming to rest on his shoulder, a gentle weight to soothe the turmoil raging within him.

"I felt the same." She sighed, and he could hear a new lightness in her voice. "But then I remembered Moira's letter, and I knew that he was meant for us."

Alastair's eyes closed, and he gripped the armrests of the chair tightly as his thoughts returned to the one sentence that had been haunting him since the day their guests had arrived.

On the day marked by a blue flower, she will find a great love up by the ruins.

Could that be what Moira had seen? Or felt?

The boy?

Pushing to his feet, Alastair looked down at the sleeping child, remembering the letter he had only received the day they had all but stumbled upon Miss Harmon and her new-born son. Moira had written to him about a new dream. A dream in which she had seen him happy, knowing that there could be no happiness for him without Deidre by his side.

Was this little boy the way by which her vision would come to pass?

His hand reached out and brushed gently over the lad's auburn curls. "Like Rory," he whispered, and his heart ached at the thought of his daughter. Longing and fear tugged at him, and he knew not what he wanted.

What he feared.

What he needed.

What he ought to do.

Deidre sighed, leaning into him, and his arm rose to settle upon her shoulders. "'Tis not a betrayal," she whispered, "to love another child for it doesna mean ye love her any less." Tears thickened her voice. "He's all alone, longing for someone to love him. In that, we are the same." Her finger caressed the boy's soft cheek before she caught the tip of a red curl between her fingers. "I feel as though Rory sent him to us, gave him her red hair so we'd know he was to be ours."

Tears streamed down Alastair's face as he wrapped his wife and child in a tight embrace, whispering a silent thank-you to his bonny, little lass for watching over them.

Forever would she be missed.

And remembered.

The Yuletide log burnt in the large hearth in the great hall, sending waves of warmth through the tall-ceilinged chamber. The scent of pine hung in the air, mingling with the delicious smells of pastries, hearty as well as sweet, which Cook had prepared for the holidays. Children dashed around the hall, their little voices cheerful and filled with awe as they gazed at the evergreen boughs as well as the stars and ribbons with which they had decorated them.

Deidre stood off to the side, her eyes no doubt possessing an equally revering glow as she watched her family's joy at this Christmas season. Her own heart beat steady and strong; but every once in a while, she could feel it perform a little somersault as though it could not contain its joy.

Sighing, Deidre turned her gaze to the sweet, little boy in her arms, his big blue eyes looking up at her. One of his hands had managed to snag a curl of her dark brown hair, keeping it clutched in his little fist. Occasionally, he would yank on it as though to get her attention, a mischievous grin on his face. "Ye're exactly like yer big sister, little Rowan," Deidre cooed at him, tickling him under the chin. "She was a wicked one herself."

Rowan gurgled happily and gave her hair another tug.

"He is beautiful."

Looking up, Deidre met John's gaze as he came to stand beside her, his eyes drifting down to Rowan, who once more yanked on her hair. "Aye, he is. He's all that and more."

A warm smile came to John's face. "I know now what you meant," he said quietly before gazing across the hall to where Tillie sat with Adelaide, her nimble fingers working on yet another straw figurine. Every day for as long as Sophie had been abed, not yet strong enough to rise, little Tillie had made her a different little ornament to decorate her chamber and help her feel better. "She's not mine," he whispered, "not truly, and yet..."

"She is," Deidre finished for him.

Their eyes met, and he smiled at her. "Yes, she is." His gaze drifted down to Rowan. "I suppose not everyone becomes a parent in the same way." A smile tickled his lips as his gaze moved up to meet hers. "Sometimes parent and child find each other in rather unexpected ways."

"Aye, 'tis true," Deidre exclaimed whole-heartedly. "Will ye stay in her life then? For good?"

John nodded. "I've never been there for her-not truly-because I always thought it was not my place. But I can no longer deny that I want to. Whether I'm her father or her uncle does not matter. She matters, and I will get to know her better. The way I should've from the beginning." A deep smile claimed his features. "It's my New Year's resolution."

Deidre laughed, "'Tis a bit early for that, but I dunna believe I've ever heard a better one."

As John crossed the hall and sat down beside Tillie, offering her his assistance with her latest creation, Deidre caught her husband's gaze. He stood with Connor in the far corner by the hearth, and the moment their eyes met, Deidre felt a tug that stole her breath.

Not on her hair.

But on her heart.

Her body hummed with the need to be near him, reawakening to an old longing that had gotten lost over the past two years. Their gazes held, locked on one another, and she watched him mumble something absentmindedly to Connor before his feet began to move, carrying him toward her. She could feel him draw closer with each step, her heart jumping and bouncing with excitement and anticipation like a young lass's in love for the first time.

Always had she felt like this in Alastair's presence, and never again would she allow herself to forget.

Or him.

"Ye look happy," he murmured, his eyes equally radiant as they moved from her to their son, still happily pulling on her hair. "Ye're aglow with warmth and love."

Deidre smiled, moving closer until he reached out, pulling her against him. "I do love ye," she whispered against his lips, a teasing smile coming to her face when his breath caught. "I love ye both." Her gaze drifted down to the contented baby in her arms, his eyelids once more growing heavy, her hair still clutched possessively in his fist.

"I love ye as well," Alastair murmured, and his arm held her tighter, one hand brushing over Rowan's little head. "I never thought I would ever feel like this again."

Deidre sighed, "If it hadna been for Moira..."

Her husband drew in a deep breath, and she could feel a slight tremor run down his arm. "Aye, she fought for us."

Deidre nodded, knowing how hard it was for Alastair to see shades of grey in the world instead of only black and white. She knew he missed his sister dearly, and yet, in all these years, he had not been able to move past her betrayal. Doubt had lingered, and he had been afraid to place his trust in her again, to be hurt again. But perhaps now...

"Aye, perhaps 'tis time," he finally whispered, his blue gaze seeking hers. "Her son is almost a year old already, and I have never even met him." He glanced at Rowan. "They're cousins, family, and they should be close."

Tears misted Deidre's eyes, and still she could not help but smile. "Aye, we're family. Sometimes we get lost, but we always find each other again."

"Always," Alastair agreed, his strong arms wrapping them in a warm embrace. It was Deidre's favourite place in the world. One she had lost once but found again.

Always.

Epilogue

Seann Dachaigh Tower
Home of Clan MacDrummond
Spring 1812

S *eann Dachaigh* Tower stood like a fortress against the grey sky, its tall walls protecting those within. Years earlier, Alastair had ridden over this small hill, his eyes falling on the imposing structure, to deliver his sister to their mother's clan.

Banishment had been her punishment for betraying her own kin.

Exile.

And yet, Moira had found a home here. She had found love with the clan's laird, Cormag MacDrummond, and step by step conquered the hearts of his people.

Alastair remembered well the way his own heart had felt that day as though it was being pulled apart. Of course, he had been furious, disappointed, broken at learning of her betrayal, and yet, his heart had never ceased loving her. It had made his anger harder to bear, and he had hoped to ease his suffering by banishing her not only from within their clan's midst but also from his thoughts, if not from his heart.

Still, it had been a daily struggle, and a part of him felt utter relief at finding himself back here.

"She'll be waiting," Deidre whispered gently, seated atop her white mare, their son strapped to her back, his little head resting against her shoulder, eyes closed in peaceful slumber.

Alastair nodded. "Aye."

Slowly, they made their way down the slope, Alastair's gaze fixed on the front gate where people moved in and out between the keep and the village surrounding it. Spring had brought rain and fog as temperatures had risen, warming the ground and making it useful once more. Fields needed tending, and the livestock now grazed contentedly upon the green hills.

Crossing through the stone archway into the courtyard, Alastair found his hands trembling with anticipation. For so long, he had refused all Moira's attempts at reconciliation. Would she welcome him now? He wondered how the letter Deidre had sent ahead of them, announcing their arrival, had been received.

"Dunna worry," his wife counselled, a compassionate smile upon her face as she gently slid out of the saddle. "Moira loves ye. She's been wishing for a reunion for years. She willna bite yer head off." A soft chuckle escaped her lips as she moved toward him. "Will ye help me with Rowan?"

After handing their horse's reins to a stable boy, Alastair turned to his wife, unfastening the chequered cloth they had used to secure Rowan upon his mother's back. The boy loved to be close, and the rhythmic swaying of the horse always had him sleeping in no time. Connor often joked that the lad would learn to ride before learning to walk.

With Rowan securely atop her arm, Deidre held out a hand to him. "Come. It willna do ye any good standing out here wondering."

Alastair nodded, then gathered his wife and son close and together they headed up the stairs leading into the great hall. The dimmer light inside momentarily had him blinking his eyes before he took note of the tall, dark-haired man sliding out of the shadows and coming toward them.

Cormag MacDrummond.

Moira's husband.

"Welcome to *Seann Dachaigh* Tower," he greeted them with a bit of a formal bow, his voice ringing with calm authority. Alastair could feel the man's gaze sweeping over him in appraisal, and he noted the protectiveness in his stance as though he felt the need to assure that this visit would not upset the woman he had married.

The woman he loved, Alastair concluded, finding himself reminded of none other than himself when it came to Deidre.

Her happiness.

Her safety.

For a long moment, the two men looked at one another before Cormag drew in a slow breath as though he had reached a decision. "Moira hasna slept a wink all night," he finally said, the hint of a smile coming to his otherwise stoic features, "and she's been pacing all morning. I wouldna be surprised if she's already worn a hole into the carpet."

Beside him, Deidre laughed, the sound of her warm voice easing Alastair's tension. "Aye, like sister, like brother."

Cormag nodded to her. "Follow me," he said, then strode off, crossing the hall and disappearing through an arched doorway.

With his wife's arm clutched at his side, Alastair followed, his gaze drifting down to Deidre's again and again.

"All will be well," she whispered, bouncing Rowan gently, who was looking about himself with big eyes.

Then they stepped inside what appeared to be a small drawing room, and the moment Alastair's gaze fell on his sister, he could have wept with joy.

With her golden tresses flowing freely down her back, she stood in the middle of the room, her blue eyes wide, staring at him as much as he was staring at her. Her cheeks shone rosy, flushed with warmth or perhaps excitement. He only hoped not with trepidation; however, the look of utter longing on her face instantly silenced his fears.

Belatedly, Alastair realised that she was holding a little boy in her arms, his hair as dark as his father's, his eyes the same startling blue as Moira's. The lad too was staring at the newcomers before Cormag moved to his wife's side, taking their son from her arms.

Alastair felt Deidre step away, his eyes still fixed on his sister. Her jaw trembled, and he could see her blinking her lashes frantically as she pressed her lips together to hold back the emotions that danced across her face.

Alastair felt it too, the overwhelming love, the desperate longing, the utter relief to find their way back to each other. "Moira," he whispered, taking another step into the room, and before he knew it, she all but flew forward and flung herself into his arms.

The impact rocked him backwards onto his heels, and choked laughter spilled from his lips as he held her tightly, relief warming his limbs. Sobs tore from her throat as she clung to him, her arms squeezing his shoulders as though she was afraid he would disappear into thin air.

Long moments ticked by as brother and sister held each other. Alastair was dimly aware of Deidre's voice as she spoke to Cormag in hushed tones. He heard Rowan squeal once or twice, interspersed by another sweet little voice.

Rowan's cousin Liam.

Moira's son.

Alastair's nephew.

Family.

"I've missed ye as well, *leannan*," Alastair whispered into his sister's hair. "It's been too long."

Sniffling, she pulled back, her blue eyes still brimming with tears. "Aye, too long." Her gaze swept over his face, noting the frown lines he had not had before as well as those caused by laughter and happiness. "Never again," she mumbled, a hint of doubt still in her voice.

Alastair nodded. "Never again."

A luminous smile danced across her face, and she hugged him again. "Now, show me yer son."

Alastair laughed. "Only if ye show me yers."

As though nothing had happened, as though no years stood between them, they fell back into their old roles, teasing and laughing as they always had. After all, they were brother and sister still. That would never change. No matter what.

Family was forever.

THE END

Thank you for reading *Haunted & Revered!*

In the next installment, *Fooled & Enlightened - The Englishman's Scottish Wife*, Maggie MacDrummond finds herself confronted by a man of her past when she returns to England upon her husband's death. Long ago, she lost her heart to Nathan Penhale, Earl of Townsend, only to have it crushed at the first test of devotion. However, not all is as it seems, and Maggie realises that she too has made mistakes.

Is it too late now?

Read a Sneak-Peek

Fooled & Enlightened
The Englishman's Scottish Wife
(#5 Highland Tales)

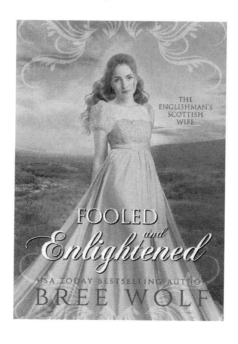

Prologue

SEANN DACHAIGH TOWER, SCOTTISH HIGHLANDS,
SUMMER 1802 (OR A VARIATION THEREOF)

TEN YEARS EARLIER

"It is breath-taking!" Margaret sighed as she stood high up on the walkway of *Seann Dachaigh* Tower, her auburn curls dancing on the strong breeze that swept over the Highlands. Her eyes widened at the sight before her, the endless rolling hills of Scotland, lush and green, the blue horizon, wide and all-encompassing, and the magical glow that made everything look brighter, more vibrant, more alive somehow. Indeed, despite her eighteen years, Lady Margaret Brandley, daughter to the Earl of Tynham, felt like a fairy as she twirled in a small circle, her feet barely touching the hard brick of the ancient fortress as the wind tugged on her green skirts. "This is heaven!"

A chuckle brought her movements to an abrupt halt, and she spun to find that she was no longer alone up on the walkway that overlooked the land in all directions.

A young man stood near the door she'd come through earlier, his blond hair glistening in the summer sun as his blue eyes-the same colour as her own-swept over her in obvious delight. Margaret would have rebuked him instantly for secretly watching her if it had not been for the warm smile lingering on his lips. He was tall and broad, and yet, the look in his eyes held nothing but kindness.

"Are ye the English lass arrived from London?" he asked, in that Highland brogue that always felt like a caress. "Lady Margaret?" His blue eyes flashed teasingly as he strode closer. "Or can I call ye Maggie?"

Unable not to, Margaret smiled at him. "You assume correctly," she told him as he came to stand next to her, his gaze momentarily sweeping over the land. "And, yes, you may call me Maggie under one condition." Indeed, Margaret could not deny that *Maggie* sounded wonderful, especially the way he pronounced it for it all but rolled off his tongue.

"And what is that?" he asked, turning to look at her with curious eyes.

The lingering warmth in his gaze was utterly endearing and it did not fail to remind her of Nathan; Nathan Penhale, Earl of Townsend, the boy she'd loved all her life.

Growing up on neighbouring country estates, they'd become close friends and allies in their search for adventure early on. Even when they'd reached a certain age and her parents had begun to discourage the intimate friendship they'd shared-considering they were of the opposite sex-they'd never lost each other. Nathan had always smuggled teasing letters into her chamber, and Margaret had answered each and every one of them. They'd met in the stables or at the lake. He'd taught her how to fence, and she'd taught him how to dance. They'd sat out by the water's edge and read to each other or played cards until sunset. Nathan knew every secret she'd ever kept, except one.

That she loved him.

That she'd loved him for as long as she could remember.

That she always would.

Sighing, Margaret urged her thoughts to return to the here and now and met the young man's enquiring gaze. "Tell me *your* name," she said with a grin.

A cheerful laugh spilled from his lips. "Aye, I havena yet, have I?"

Rubbing his chin, he squinted against the sun before his gaze moved back to her. "Ian. Ian MacDrummond."

"'Tis nice to meet ye, Ian," Margaret greeted him, trying to say the words the way he did.

Beaming at her, Ian laughed. "D'ye wish to be a Scot then, Maggie?"

Gazing out at the green land around her, Margaret sighed. "I never thought of it. My mother is from here, and she's always told me stories about the Highlands." She cast a look at him sideways as they leaned onto the parapet wall side by side. "I always knew that she missed it. Sometimes she even had tears in her eyes when she spoke of her life here."

"Then why did she leave?" Ian asked, a hint of incredulity in his eyes.

Margaret laughed as a part of her understood the urge to remain in this place forever. She hadn't until she'd come here a few weeks ago, but now she did. "Because she was in love," she told Ian with a roll of her eyes.

"Yer father?"

Margaret nodded. "Aye," she said grinning, and he smiled at her.

"Then this is only a visit?" he asked, and she could see his eyes dim a little. "Ye're going home at the end of summer?"

Margaret sighed. "It is beautiful here," she whispered with a longing glance at the green hills surrounding her, "and I understand now why my mother loves it so..."

"But?"

Margaret cast him a quick smile. "But my life is back in England."

His brows drew down, but the hint of a smile remained on his face. "Yer life?" he asked, and a teasing curl came to his lips that reminded her of Nathan. "Or rather yer heart?"

Feeling her cheeks flush red hot, Margaret turned her head away, but could not deny the joy that danced in her heart at the thought of Nathan.

Of the altogether unexpected kiss they'd shared the night before her departure.

"'Tis as I suspected," Ian declared rather triumphantly. "'Twould seem ye and yer mother are very much alike."

The door at their backs creaked open in that moment and footsteps followed them out onto the walkway. "Oh, there ye are, my dear," came her mother's voice, her accent thickening with each day that they spent in Scotland. "And Wee Ian," she exclaimed as she stepped toward them and the wind gathered up her auburn hair-the same as Margaret's.

Beside her, Ian chuckled. "I'm not so wee anymore."

Smiling at him, her mother shook her head in awe. "I always pictured ye as a wee laddie after your mother's letters. She wrote so often about ye that I felt certain I'd know ye the moment I saw ye." Her smile deepened, with only a hint of wistfulness to it. "And I was right."

Ian swallowed. "She woulda loved to see ye again, Lady Tynham," he told her mother. "She always spoke of ye."

Margaret saw her mother's gaze mist with tears at the thought of her old friend. "I'll never forget her, and I'm happy to be back here and see ye." Her gaze swept over him from head to toe. "A giant now!" Laughter spilled from her lips, and Ian laughed with her. "I'm glad ye've finally returned from yer travels. We must speak further," she told him with a sidelong glance at Margaret, "but would ye grant me a moment with my daughter first? There's something I need to speak to her about."

Ian nodded. "Of course." Then he turned to look at Margaret. "'Tis been a pleasure to meet ye, *Maggie*."

Margaret smiled at him before he strode away, and yet, she shivered as an odd chill chased itself down her back. "What is it, Mother?" she asked, noting the slight strain on her mother's face as she came to stand beside her. "Is something wrong?"

Her mother sighed, a deep, long sigh that said more than a thousand words. "I received a letter from Lady Barkley," she began and her gaze moved from Scotland's rolling hills to settle on her young daughter. "She wrote to me about a certain development, which...I fear will be...hard for ye to hear."

Margaret swallowed, and her arms wrapped around herself as the wind suddenly felt cold. Ice-cold. "What is it, Mother? Tell me." But did she truly wish to know?

Her mother's eyes closed before she reached out and grasped her daughter's hands, pulling them into her own. "An engagement has been announced."

Margaret stared into her mother's blue eyes, and she knew without a doubt what it was her mother was not saying. "N-Nathan?" Margaret stammered as her eyes filled with tears.

Squeezing her daughter's hands, Lady Tynham nodded. "I'm so sorry, my dear. I know ye must be heartbroken. I know how much ye cared for him."

Tears streamed freely down Margaret's cheeks as she stared at her mother, wishing with every fibre of her being that this was a nightmare. Nothing more. "It's not p-possible," she sobbed. "It has to be a m-mistake."

Her mother shook her head. "I'm afraid 'tis not. The date has been set. All of London knows. 'Tis not a mistake."

As tears streamed down her face like a flood pouring from the heavens, Margaret knew not what to do with the pain slowly ripping a hole into her heart. "I-I h-have to speak to h-him," she sobbed, her jaw trembling with the emotions assaulting her so unexpectedly she could barely speak. "I n-need him to t-tell me w-why-"

"No," her mother interrupted, her eyes kind and compassionate while her lips thinned in determination. "He's made his choice, my dear, and he's made it known to the world. Nothing ye say will sway him now. It'll only serve to humiliate ye, to break yer heart further." She brushed a gentle hand over her daughter's cheek, her touch comforting, but not healing as it once had been when Margaret had been a little girl. This was a pain her mother could not chase away. "He's always ever been yer friend. He never spoke to ye of love, did he?"

Gritting her teeth against the all-consuming sobs that rose in her throat, Margaret looked up at her mother, unable not to hate her in this moment-at least a little-for pointing out the truth. "No," she finally confessed. "He never did."

Her mother nodded, then pulled Margaret into her arms. "I know ye're hurting, my dear, and I know it doesna feel like it right now, but I promise ye it'll pass. With time, it'll pass."

Clinging to her mother, Margaret pressed her eyes shut, wishing she could retreat from the world, suddenly so harsh and painful. "But he kissed me," she whispered into her mother's hair. "Before we left, he kissed me."

Her mother sighed. "Perhaps 'twas a kiss goodbye."

Margaret had never thought such pain was possible. Her insides felt as though they were being ripped apart, as though her whole body was battered and bruised, and she could barely stand.

How could she have been so wrong? Had she misunderstood a friendly kiss for something deeper? Why had Nathan not said a word? As her friend at least he ought to have told her he intended to marry, ought he not?

Standing back, her mother gently brushed the tears from her eyes, a soft smile on her lips as she looked into Margaret's eyes. "We'll stay in Scotland for a wee bit longer," she whispered, "so we willna be back in London for the wedding."

Her mother's words felt like someone had reached inside her chest and torn her heart out.

Nathan's wedding.

To another.

"We'll stay here," her mother continued, gently tucking a stray curl behind Margaret's ear. "It'll be good for ye to get a little distance, to give yer heart time to heal."

A soft neigh drifted to their ears, and they turned to see Ian ride out of the front gate down into the meadows surrounding the village. Halfway down the path, he turned in his saddle and looked up at them, then raised a hand to wave.

Margaret couldn't move. Her eyes stared in shock at such a normal, every-day gesture; a normal, every-day gesture that seemed impossible for her to return. Nothing was as it had been moments ago. Everything had changed, and she knew not what to do about it, how to continue on.

Putting on a smile, her mother waved back and they watched as Ian spurred his mount on and charged across the meadow toward the small stream cutting through the land. "He's a good lad," her mother remarked before she turned to look at her daughter. "I know it doesna seem possible right now, but one day yer heart will be able to love another. Just ye wait. It'll happen," she squeezed Margaret's hand, "if ye allow it to look elsewhere."

Margaret closed her eyes and felt another tear roll down her cheek as her heart broke into a thousand pieces.

Series Overview

LOVE'S SECOND CHANCE: TALES OF LORDS & LADIES

LOVE'S SECOND CHANCE: TALES OF DAMSELS & KNIGHTS

LOVE'S SECOND CHANCE: HIGHLAND TALES

FORBIDDEN LOVE SERIES

HAPPY EVER REGENCY SERIES

THE WHICKERTONS IN LOVE

For more information visit www.breewolf.com

About Bree

USA Today bestselling and award-winning author, Bree Wolf has always been a language enthusiast (though not a grammarian!) and is rarely found without a book in her hand or her fingers glued to a keyboard. Trying to find her way, she has taught English as a second language, traveled abroad and worked at a translation agency as well as a law firm in Ireland. She also spent loooong years obtaining a BA in English and Education and an MA in Specialized Translation while wishing she could simply be a writer. Although there is nothing simple about being a writer, her dreams have finally come true.

"A big thanks to my fairy godmother!"

Currently, Bree has found her new home in the historical romance genre, writing Regency novels and novellas. Enjoying the mix of fact and fiction, she occasionally feels like a puppet master (or mistress? Although that sounds weird!), forcing her characters into ever-new situations that will put their strength, their beliefs, their love to the test, hoping that in the end they will triumph and get the happily-ever-after we are all looking for.

If you're an avid reader, sign up for Bree's newsletter on **www. breewolf.com** as she has the tendency to simply give books away. Find out about freebies, giveaways as well as occasional advance reader copies and read before the book is even on the shelves!

Connect with Bree and stay up-to-date on new releases:

facebook.com/breewolf.novels

twitter.com/breewolf_author

instagram.com/breewolf_author

amazon.com/Bree-Wolf/e/B00FJX27Z4

bookbub.com/authors/bree-wolf

Printed in Great Britain
by Amazon

41411997R10065